making the run

making the run

a novel

heather henson

JOANNA COTLER BOOKS
An Imprint of HarperCollins*Publishers*

Jacket photos, clockwise from top left:
© 2001 Jonathon Safir / Photonica;
© 2001 Tatsuyo Morita / Photonica;
© 2001 Robert Discalfani / Photonica;
© 2001 Jonathon Safir / Photonica.

Making the Run
Printed in the United States of America. For information address HarperCollins
Children's Books, a division of HarperCollins Publishers,
1350 Avenue of the Americas, New York, NY 10019.
www.harperteen.com

Library of Congress Cataloging-in-Publication Data
Henson, Heather.
   Making the run : a novel / by Heather Henson.
      p.   cm.
   Summary: Eighteen-year-old Lu is set on leaving her Kentucky home town
after high school graduation, but her plans are complicated by friends and
family, old grief, and new love.
   ISBN 0-06-029796-4 — ISBN 0-06-029797-2 (lib. bdg.)
   [1. Coming of age—Fiction.   2. Friendship—Fiction.   3. Love—Fiction.
4. Fathers and daughters—Fiction.   5. Kentucky—Fiction.]   I. Title.
PZ7.H39863 Mak   2002   2001039870
[Fic]—dc21   CIP
                                                                       AC

Typography by Alicia Mikles
1 2 3 4 5 6 7 8 9 10
❖
First HarperTempest edition, 2002

for tim: my love-at-first-sight

deepest gratitude to: jane lazarre for setting me firmly on the road many years ago and for continuing to be a guiding light; eben and charlotte henson for raising me to follow my dreams; robby, holly, eben jr. and jan henson for going first and paving the way with love and creative energy; joanna cotler for her generosity and insight; daniel walker ungs for giving me a deadline and a crazy kind of love.

making the run

"It made me think that everything was about to arrive—the moment when you know it all and everything is decided forever."

—Jack Kerouac, *On the Road*

It happened when I was just a little girl. My mother dying. I was there. I saw it, although I don't remember anything except colors. Red and purple, yellow and green. And blue—everywhere—a deep, endless blue. It was early summer. The colors were her garden. Roses and irises, tulips and daffodils. Grass and sky. I don't remember screaming, although I've been told I screamed myself voiceless, the noise bringing Danny and then the neighbors and then the ambulance with the wail loud enough to finally drown me out. It didn't change anything—the people, the ambulance. My mother died before my very eyes, and that's what they say made me who I am. The trouble, the bad grades, the problem with authority figures (namely my father), the willfulness. It all came from that moment I saw my mother fall forward into her beloved flowers, never to get up and hold me again, wipe away my tears. My beautiful, laughing mother. Suddenly so quiet and so still. Something bursting inside her brain. A tiny time bomb waiting all her life to go off. A death just waiting to happen.

And sometimes, when I'm trying to remember the things that came before—the feel of her breath against my cheek, the sound of her voice saying my name—I start thinking about what's underneath my own skin. I start wondering what's inside me, ticking, ready to go off.

1

"Dead Man. We're coming up to Dead Man."

Ginny makes the announcement and I feel her easing on the brakes, taking it slow. Respectful silence as we come around the bend. We know kids just like us have lost their lives here. We know the road from Rainey to Huntsville is washed in blood. Little white crosses with faded ribbons blowing in the breeze. Shrines to loved ones lost.

Crazy when you think about it. Risking your life just for a bottle of booze. But Rainey is a small town and it's a Saturday night. What else is there to do?

The road goes straight again and Ginny right away brings us back up to speed. The wind coming at us through the windows wipes it all away. Any kind of worry. Without a second thought I slip my hand into my bag. The sun is almost gone but it's an instant reflex. Camerahead, my father calls me because I always have the lens attached to my face.

Ginny looks sideways for a split second, her golden curls whipping around her face, her mouth open in a partway grin, and I snap.

ginny: making the run

I like to give a name to what I see. I have a whole Ginny series on my darkroom wall at home, my gallery I call it. Pictures going back at least four years, since this old Nikon became a part of me.

ginny: catching the breeze
ginny: getting crazy
ginny: hitting the hard stuff

I have a whole series of kids from school, friends and relatives, Kentucky roads—blacktop winding off into nowhere.

"I could make this run in thirty-five flat," Ginny says above the rushing air and the music blasting from the speakers.

I shake my head. Ginny's car is a fast little turbo, but Rainey to Huntsville is forty-five miles of twisting and turning. There's ninety-degree Dead Man's Curve to contend with and other nips and tucks to slow things down. No way to do it in less than fifty. Longer

4

when you get behind some slow-moving junker.

"I could make this run blindfolded," she tries again.

This time I nod my head.

"Maybe so."

I'm thinking that maybe most people in Rainey could make this run blindfolded. The road to salvation, Danny calls it. The nearest place for quenching your thirst. Rainey may be a dry town but that doesn't mean nobody's tipping the bottle. It just means people go to crazy lengths to get wasted.

The road begins to wind down, taking us toward the river. A wetness is filling up the car. New leaves and flowers blooming.

"Do you smell that?" I want to know.

Ginny sniffs at the air, an obedient puppy dog, but comes up blank.

"Summer." I help her out. "It smells like summer. Already."

Ginny raises two fingers in the air. "Countdown to freedom."

I turn back toward the window, satisfied. Two

months to go. Graduation, my eighteenth birthday, freedom. My father thinks I'm going to the University of Kentucky like most of the other college-bound Rainey High grads, lambs to the slaughter. But I've got some money saved and I've got other plans.

Outside is a quick blur of dark and light. Trees and sky. Pointless to take a picture, but I lean way out the window anyway and watch the motion through my lens. Lots of times I don't even click. I just like to look at things through the eye of the camera. I like the way things can be boxed in, separated out, contained.

"Okay, Lu." Ginny goes serious when we cross the county line. "I hope you're ready to get wild because that's what it's about tonight."

I nod my head. I know the plan. I don't have any problem with it.

In the Barn parking lot Ginny brushes out her hair and puts on lipstick. She's always the one to go in because she can pass for twenty-one. She has her fake ID just in case. But you never know, even with a fake or borrowed ID. Sometimes the Barn guys like to give kids a hard time just to make the time pass quicker.

The parking lot is lit up like Christmas. Neon signs advertising every kind of beer. One big sign proclaiming the Barn's status as first and last wet stop in these parts. The cars are streaming in. Everybody's doing their Saturday night run, same as us. I hang out the window, watching the kids pull in. Kids who look even younger than we are, trying to act like it's no big deal. Through the lens I frame a line of cars, the neon lights bouncing off the hoods like a rainbow. I know the shutter will be slow in this light so I hold the camera real still.

huntsville: saturday night

After a few minutes Ginny comes sashaying across the blacktop, two paper bags held out like trophies. All the young hopefuls watch her with envy.

"Score." She puts the big bag in the trunk. The smaller bag she brings up front and sets at my feet. As soon as we're on the road again, she gets me to open a pint of Jack. In the dark she takes a hard pull and the bottle goes back and forth between us. My body gives a shiver every time the whiskey goes down. I'm not sure I'll ever get used to the burning, like swallowing fire. But Ginny swigs the stuff like it's water.

"It's in my veins," she'll say when she's truly wiped. "I was practically weaned on the stuff." And she'll be speaking the truth because I've never seen her mama or daddy without a drink in their hands.

Ginny turns the music way up for the rewind back to Rainey.

"Invincible," she yells as she floors it, shooting us past the more timid drivers. "I am invincible."

After a few hits off the bottle I close my eyes. The whiskey is making me numb and cozy. I could stay this way all night. Moving fast and feeling nothing. This is what I've been doing all year. Getting high, marking time. This day next year I don't know where I'll be. But I can guarantee it won't be here, on the road between Huntsville and Rainey.

After a while I feel the car slow down. My eyes pop open to the WELCOME TO RAINEY sign. Big and cheerful. An ENJOY YOUR STAY! written in bubbly type at the bottom. As if droves of tourists are making their way to Rainey, Kentucky, just to enjoy themselves. As if Rainey is anything more than a gas stop along the way to somewhere else: Knoxville to the south and Lexington to the north.

"Cheese it, coppers." Ginny slows down to the lawful speed limit and reaches for the Chloroseptic she keeps in the glove compartment.

The key when coming back from a run is to observe all the laws carefully. Don't go too slow or too fast. Don't run any red lights and don't scoot through yellows. Come to a complete stop at the four-ways. Look like you are a law-abiding citizen even though you are seventeen with an open bottle of Jack between your knees.

Ginny passes all the tests and shoots us onto the bypass. On the other side of town there's the Wal-Mart parking lot with a bunch of cars at one dark corner, just like every other Saturday night. One more ritual I won't miss when I'm gone. All the same faces, the same waiting around and talking loud and trying to guess when the cops are going to make their next sweep so that you have to scatter to the next hangout spot—the Piggly Wiggly parking lot or, if it's late enough, Rounders, the hidden waterfall on the river.

"I won't miss this." I say it out loud. "I won't miss this when I'm gone."

Ginny turns to me and even in the dark I can tell she's giving me her patented pout, the one that works like a charm on her daddy when she's done something wrong.

"I asked you. I asked you if you were ready to get wild, Lu."

"Yeah, I know. It's just—" Hard to explain to Ginny, even with knowing her practically my whole life. Hard to explain because this is her world, her crowd. She's looking forward to heading to UK in the fall, a sweet little lamb. Sometimes I wonder why everything is so difficult. For me. "It's just." I try again. "Aren't you tired of this? Aren't you tired of it all?"

Ginny stops the car at the edge of the circle and leans over to wrestle her beloved Jack from my grip.

"Loner Lu." Taking a neat sip. "Why do you come out then? Why do you bother?"

I shrug. Hard to explain that part even to myself.

"A moth to the flame," I answer.

Ginny laughs and then wraps her fingers tight around my wrist.

"What holds us together? What do you think?"

I look down at her nails biting into my skin. New paint—ice blue. I think I know what holds us together, what keeps us together in our free time even when we go our separate ways at school. Ginny hanging with the jocks and the preps and the country club kids, doing the wild thing on the weekends just to prove something to herself. Me with nothing to prove, hanging with the stoners and the freaks, getting high morning, noon and night as a way to make it through to freedom. I think I know what holds us together but I'm not going to say, and she doesn't want me to anyway because she's already dropping my arm, turning away from me to get on with her Saturday night.

"Hey baby, just in time." Taylor Boyd leans into

the window, all teeth and football-star charm. And since Taylor's there, Wade Sparks isn't far behind, reaching his hands into the back of the car, feeling around, a mad frenzy for booze.

"I can smell it," Wade says. "But I don't see it."

Ginny releases the trunk, and Taylor is already passing the cans of beer around. Pacified, Wade opens my door and squats down in front of me. He's on a mission lately to figure me out, get me inside his Jeep Cherokee. A notch on his belt before graduation.

"Cool," Wade says, looking me up and down in a slow take. "Out of this world."

I sip my beer without saying a word. I know Wade is only mocking. He doesn't get the short hair or the tiny silver loop piercing my eyebrow or the old clothes I wear. Vintage and usually black. Dead people's clothes.

"Hey, Lu, you got some of that funky stuff?"

What he does get is my status as smoker. It means I'm usually holding.

"Yeah, but I'm not doing it here."

"I know, I know. But later. You know, maybe before the party."

"Maybe."

Holding weed. It's one of the things I'm good for in this crowd. The preps and the jocks are fraidy-cats when it comes to buying stuff on their own. Might ruin their supposedly spotless reputations. But they don't mind taking a few hits from me on occasion. Ginny is the same way. She drinks like a fish, and she's been known to get stoned with me once or twice, but she can also get up on her high horse about my smoking.

I push past Wade so I don't have to smell his Polo cologne and his beer breath up close. With the dark settled in, the promise of summer is gone. It could be fall again, the air cool and crisp. I lean onto the heated-up hood of the car for a little warmth. Wade is there before I can settle back and enjoy the stars washing across the sky. His hand wraps around my ankle, then makes a slow sweep up to the knee. I close my eyes, try to separate the hand from the body. Being touched makes something happen. No matter who it is. The skin tingles just a little, the face flushes the tiniest bit. I store this away for future use. Like a scientist making a scientific observation. For a millisecond I wonder what he would do. If I gave in. I wonder if there'd be panic or smooth moves.

"Hey baby," Wade whispers, sensing some kind of hesitation.

I slide my hand into my bag and push the camera between us. No guy is worth the risk. Opening myself up, naked. Not in this town. Through the lens Wade is just a dark silhouette, insignificant.

The dark silhouette laughs and pulls his hand away. It's only a game. He thinks persistence will get him somewhere in the end.

"Did that hurt?" He tries to reach around the camera to my face ring.

"You know, you're totally wasted. You ask me that every time you're totally wasted."

"It's just, you know, it looks like it would be painful."

"Sometimes a little pain isn't such a bad thing."

Wade's blue eyes go wide and then he laughs again, a big, sloppy laugh.

"Wacked, you know you are so wacked." He's all the way slurring now. "But I like you." He leans around the lens and gets this look on his face like he's doing me a favor and I don't know it yet. "Crazy, you know, that's what people call you, right? Sometimes. Crazy Lu."

There are times this kind of thing can put me into a tailspin, a dizzy dive into out of control. Blind rage, one counselor called it. Residual anger from feelings of abandonment (my mother's death). I still have the Xeroxed sheet that M.S.W. (no Ph.D.) gave me. Ten Steps to Dealing with Anger in a Positive Way. But tonight I'm the one who's laughing. As if I need Wade Sparks to tell me about my own life. As if I don't know that living in a small town is like living under a microscope. Every little thing magnified and studied, notes taken. Judgments made.

Wade is surprised by my laughter. He pulls himself up, all sincerity.

"Sometimes I worry about you, Lu."

"Don't." I stop laughing and put the camera away. "A few weeks to go and you won't have to think about me at all."

Wade's face crunches up, trying to think things through.

"We got the whole summer," he says. "After graduation we got the whole summer."

I shake my head. "Not me. With me it's like some old country song—I got leaving on my mind."

Even in his drunken state, Wade sees an opening in my words. There's some study that says guys think about sex ninety-nine percent of the time, and knowing Wade, I believe it. Without the camera he comes in close, right up against my face.

"So what've you got to lose?" His hand is back on my body, running up my thigh. "A few weeks to go. We should make the most of it. What've you got to lose?"

"Her self-respect, for one."

It's Ginny, finally, coming to my rescue. She pulls me off the hood and tucks me back into the passenger side before Wade can follow the motion.

"Where you going?" Wade cries like a little boy.

"Party time," Ginny yells.

"But wait, we'll tailgate." Wade is blind in the headlights, trying to block his opponent just like he does on the football field. "Lu said she'd give me some funky stuff."

"You'll have to catch us later." Ginny revs the engine, heading us back down the bypass, through the sad, empty streets of town. After the buildings and houses have fallen away, we're turning into farmland, little lanes curling around long shadowy fields.

"I hope you can find your way back," I tell Ginny, staring out into the blackness, feeling just a little panicky, like I'm going to be swallowed up by bluegrass.

"I know the way," Ginny says. She makes a few more turns until suddenly we're on Landers Lane. The road is already lined with parked cars, shadow people weaving in and out of the headlights. Big springtime blowout on Landers' Farm.

Ginny eases into a spot under a tree but we don't get out right away. I reach for the nickel bag I got from Bunny Johnson. Ginny leans back, smoking a menthol and watching my hands rolling one for now and one for later. When I'm finished, I make an offer but Ginny shakes her head.

"You know this is *my* poison." She pats the bottle of Jack. "Aren't you worried about that stuff frying your brain?"

"I'm not worried about anything," I tell her, and maybe it's true. At least it's true right now.

We sit for a while, not talking. Just drinking and smoking, listening to the far-off sounds of the party. Voices fade in and out. A girl screams and then the scream turns into laughter. Music starts up, floating down through the trees.

"There's your brother," Ginny says.

I cock my head, trying to hear what song Orpheus, my brother's band, is playing, but the sound fades off on the breeze.

"Danny's cool," Ginny says in a quiet voice, and I know what she's thinking. She's missing her own brother, Ted, who's gone, killed when his speedboat flipped over. That was about six years ago. And this is the thing that holds us together. This is what I wouldn't say out loud before. We both know what it is to lose somebody.

"How do I look?" Ginny reaches into her bag and pulls out her compact. A little light comes on when she flips the lid. She fools with her hair, her lipstick, and then she leans in and pushes her face up close to mine.

I bat my lashes like some old southern belle. The little light makes me look freaky. Kohl lining the eyes, deep red lipstick, pale skin.

"Crazy Lu," I say to myself in the mirror.

Ginny clicks her tongue. "Don't listen to Wade. He talks out his butt half the time."

"No, I like it. Crazy Lu."

In the glass Ginny and I are like night and day. Long curly blond hair against dark brown cut short and sticking out every which way. Blue eyes against green. Ginny's mouth is this little rosebud while mine is wide and full, too big for my face. I know how much we've both changed over the past few years. I see it in the pictures on my wall at home. Ginny was always tall but now she's blossomed out, become rounder and fuller while I seem to have become smaller, more compact.

"Let's roll." Ginny tucks the bottle of Jack into her bag and we head out into the night, stumbling up the dark lane with the other shadow people.

"Shit, man, this is a party," Ginny keeps saying every few feet until her words are drowned out by a loud growl behind us. I turn into the eye of a single white beam. The bike is weaving back and forth in between the shadows and then it is already past, a roar of chrome and leather, a red dot blinking behind like a giant cigarette butt. I know I'm really high because the sight and sound remind me of something, take me back to my childhood—a time when Danny and his friends were into dirt bikes. Motocross racing on the weekends. Jumping and doing crazy eights on Old Man Seeley's back forty. The guys would take me along for fun sometimes, passing me back and forth between them, telling me to hold on tight when they went airborne. I remember the feeling. Like flying. Like I could never come down.

"Check it out." Ginny brings me back to the here and now. The party is in a big open field. The bonfire at the center makes everything ghostly, haunted. Witches and warlocks circling the flames, faces glowing and eyes like glass. Demons sitting on hay bales, watching and whispering outside the light. The music Orpheus is playing is loud and pulsing. Clusters of wannabe witches in tight jeans, teased-up hair and painted faces are huddled around the platform, staring at the guys like they could swallow them whole. Ginny joins them, but I hang back. The weed is making me watchful. One hand reaches into my bag and wraps around the lens. I know there's not enough light here, but I can see inside my head what the pictures would be.

saturday night: dark longing

Danny is in his drummer's trance. He's staring off to one side, sticks on rawhide. His long blond hair is hiding his eyes. Baby blues that drive girls crazy.

If you didn't know the story, you wouldn't guess we're related. Danny is like some surfer boy caught in a landlocked state. He radiates blond godliness, love and light. If you asked, I'd never call Danny my half brother because he's closer to me than anything whole. But that's what he is. Half brother. The only kid from my father's first marriage, before he met my mother.

One song ends and Danny counts off another right away. Ginny comes back for me and we start to sway together. She pulls me into the circle of dancers and we hold on to one another, moving with the rhythm. I can feel eyes watching us. I know we look far-out in this crowd. Even in my kickass elevating boots she towers over me. But we have the same moves—smooth and uncomplicated when the beat is mellow, raging when the beat goes hard. We like dancing together. Some weekends we use our fake IDs and head to Lexington to Johnny Angel's, the one cool dance club. We slam at each other and don't let guys cut in. But tonight Ginny is ready for action.

"Yummy," she whispers into my ear. "Check out all the guys."

One of them moves in for the kill. Ginny holds on to me for a little while longer, but then she lets go and I drift to the edge again. I'm used to the way guys fasten on to Ginny. All-American but drop-dead sexy. She's like a magnet.

At the keg I make the usual small talk with nameless zombies. Everybody's revved up for graduation. Nothing else matters. Except of course prom. Senior prom. The biggest night of most of these kids' lives. In my semistoned state I find myself spinning into a nightmare fantasy: going to the prom with Wade. I see a blue tux and some bad, up close, boner-crush dancing. And later, some heavy-handed positioning toward LeHigh, the make-out spot.

"I hooked you up, right?"

It's Bunny Johnson, his pale face looming at me in the dark. I feel his skinny arm slipping around my shoulders and squeezing me closer.

"Killer, just like you said." I smile and try to ease back just a little. Wade to Bunny in one heartbeat.

Frying pan to fire. Bunny is great at supplying but he's pretty reptilian. He has a nasty habit of trying to coax girls into blow jobs in exchange for drugs.

"You interested in something else?" Bunny asks, and I swear a little forked tongue darts out with a tiny hiss.

"What have you got?" Fearless, that's always my stance around Bunny.

"Just in." He holds his hand out for me to see. A little white pill. "I'll give you a little taste for free." His voice has gone all sweet and country as if he's talking about penny candy.

Crazy Lu. My body is already spinning, but the temptation is there. I can feel it building up inside me, my blood craving something more. Bunny pulls me in close again and I feel like one of the little white mice the science teacher, Mr. Leden, feeds to the boa constrictor he keeps in a glass case in his classroom. Stunned and prepped for digestion. Being pulled farther down into the dark, away from the light and the living.

"You kinda look like a boy with that haircut."

Bunny grins. His teeth are stained from smoking. "But that's okay." I feel his hand patting my head like I'm a good doggy. I imagine his long fingers pushing my head down into his crotch and that's what gets me out of his boa constrictor grip.

"Hey," Bunny calls. "Where you going? You're not scared, are you?"

"I'm not scared of anything," I call back, but I keep walking, following Danny's voice like a rope back to safety. He's making an announcement. Something about saying good-bye to an old friend but saying hello to a new old friend. The guys ease into a new tune, a song I haven't heard before. When I look around the crowd I see that Lloyd, the bass player, is gone and another body is standing in his place, back to the audience, playing to Danny. Medium height, thin but strong looking. There's something familiar about the way he stands, straight and tall, leaning just a little down into the bass. The back muscles ripple through a tight black T. The arms sinewy, veins popping as if the music is pulsing through his blood. Something familiar, and when he turns I know that the face is thinner and the hair is short now, but it's Jay Shepard. One of Danny's oldest friends, one of my first crushes. Jay Shepard with the cool gray eyes and the open smile that always made me feel like smiling too.

Jay steps up to the mike and his voice comes out softer than I remember. Smooth, but with a hard line underneath, an edge to cut through the bullshit. The words are about searching for something, but never finding it. The voice reels me in closer to the stage. I'm staring like some zoned-out groupie, and I'm listening and remembering too. It was Jay I used to ride with most of the time, if I wasn't riding with Danny. Way back when on Old Man Seeley's land. It was Jay who used to take me flying into the air when he did his jumps and wheelies.

Jay's voice stops, but the music surges on and I can still hear his work in the song, the bass line holding it all together. Danny taught me how to do that, to listen to what's inside the music, all the different layers that make up a song.

When I open my eyes Jay is looking right at me,

and it's like I stop breathing inside that look. My skin heats up and I want to slide back into the shadows because I know my face must be turning a terrible pink, but I'm frozen in place.

Jay's mouth opens into that old smile, the one that always made me smile when I was a little girl, and so I do now. I smile. And then the song is over and Jay is turning away, back toward Danny.

"Who's the babe?" Ginny lunges into me, stringing some guy behind her like a fish on the line.

I feel myself breathing again. Everything back to normal.

"You remember Jay Shepard." I shrug, keep it simple. "Danny's friend."

"Not really. But now he's totally memorable."

I keep watching the stage. Danny and Jay are grinning at each other, connected in the music. An old cover, a classic they used to play years ago.

"Where's he been all my life?" Ginny purrs.

Jay has the bass against his thighs, plucking at the chords. His hands look large for his body, strong, holding all that music inside them.

27

Ginny nudges me for some kind of answer, but I shake my head again. I don't know where Jay's been. All I know is he took off seven or eight years ago. He was going out west somewhere. Danny never talked about it much. He didn't say anything about Jay being back or starting in with the band again.

Ginny keeps trying to get me to dance with her, but I move into the shadows, trying to resist this strange urge to stare at Jay like some pathetic groupie chick. The music is tight tonight, the songs coming out fresh and new. Danny is grinning and it's obvious Jay is liking being back onstage. I close my eyes, listening, and then a hand grabs my arm.

"Where's Gin?"

It's Taylor. I try to turn him around, away from the dancing crowd. Damage control.

"I think she's getting a beer."

His eyes are already locked above my head. "No she's not." His face goes hard, the lips tightening into a straight line. I turn to see what he's seeing. Ginny and her catch are looking pretty intimate already.

Taylor makes a beeline and Wade goes in for the

assist. There's some shoving and Ginny's voice rises above the music. People turn to watch. The band looks up but keeps playing.

Ginny rushes out of the crowd, holding on to the new guy. Taylor tries to follow, but then he just stops and stares after them. Ginny glances around and I know she's looking for me. For some reason I slide deeper into the shadows. I know I'll need to find another ride home tonight.

At the edge of the field I run into Alix and Darrell, two of my stoner buddies from school. We follow a little path down a hill to a pond. The frogs go silent at the sound of our voices, but then one by one they start up again. Alix and Darrell are good at keeping quiet and just smoking. No small talk. The music floats down the hill, merging with the frog sound. I want to go back to the music, to watching Jay, but I think I have time.

The joint goes back and forth between us, until I'm lying in the soft grass. It's already wet with dew. I can feel it through my clothes just a little. My eyes are open, searching the dark, and Jay keeps flashing back into my mind. Little pieces like the photo-graphs I take. Gray eyes. Large hands. His voice flowing out smooth and hard at the same time. I wonder if the new song is one he wrote. I wonder if that's what his time away from Rainey amounted to. Looking for something and not finding it.

"You okay?"

It's Alix, leaning over me. I study her long skinny face with the freckles all over it. I have a few pictures of her lighting up behind the bleachers. I know what most people know. Alix is one of Bunny's blow-job survivors. I want to reach out and tell her I'm sorry.

"Shit, how long have we been down here?" I ask instead.

Alix shrugs and pulls me up.

On the road I can't hear the music anymore. There are voices around us, people leaving the party. Somebody says the cops will start making the rounds soon, checking for weavers.

I head back toward the field, hoping Danny is still there breaking down the equipment.

"Lucinda Larrimore McClellan."

The whole thing stops me dead and spins me around. Nobody calls me that. Not even my father when he's really pissed.

"It's quite a mouthful."

Even in the dark I know it's Jay. The voice pulls me closer like before. Jay is sitting on a bike. It must be the bike I saw earlier.

"I prefer Lu." I finally find my voice.

"I know. I remember. Little Lu." The name Danny calls me. I can feel Jay's eyes going up and down in the dark. Not a sleazy look, just taking it in, noting the differences. "Not so little anymore."

"Jay." It's like I'm walking through the dark in a fog. The weed has made me hazy. "Where did you come from?" I look around as if there's supposed to be some kind of time travel machine, whipping Jay back from wherever he was in space and time.

Jay pats the bike.

"Danny sold his." I move closer, feeling an urge to wrap my hands around the handlebars.

"Probably a smart thing to do." Jay says. "Thinking about doing that myself."

"Don't. I mean, I'd love to have a bike. Maybe when I leave here."

"Not long now, right?"

"Couple of months."

"Man." Jay looks off down the road. "Time flies."

"Maybe time flies outside of Rainey." I laugh. "Where'd you go anyway? Out west, right? Danny said you were out west."

Jay nods his head. "A lot of places. Out west mostly. Tucson, Albuquerque. Denver for a while."

"Cool. That must have been cool." Jay doesn't respond right away and so I rush on ahead. "I'm taking off too." Telling secrets, things I haven't told anybody except Ginny. "After graduation. I have some money saved. I want to see the world."

Jay says something and I think it's "Be careful," but it gets lost in a car engine starting up nearby. We're quiet, listening to it spin off toward the main road.

"What are you doing here?" I ask. "I mean,

Danny didn't say anything about you being back, about you being in the band."

"It happened kind of fast." Jay shrugs.

"How long are you staying?"

"Not sure. We'll see."

We're quiet again, glancing around at the other shadows leaving the party. Suddenly Jay leans in close and it makes me start back.

"Hey, what's up? What have you been smoking?" His voice is scolding but laughing too.

I feel my skin burning hot again. I don't know why it should matter. I know all about Danny and Jay getting wasted in the garage while they practiced their music. Danny never hid stuff from me. He never encouraged me either. He'd be mad to see me so high.

"I lost my lift." I shrug. "Ginny. She took off." I turn and wave my hand in the air.

Jay is smiling his old familiar smile, waiting for me to run myself out.

"Hop on then." He pats the bike.

"I was going to find Danny."

"He's got the equipment. And he's got a friend." Jay pauses and I shake my head. Danny is a heart-breaker. So is Jay, from what I remember. Always some chick hanging on his arm after a gig. "It's okay. I can take you home."

Jay hands me the extra helmet and kick starts the bike. The noise takes away my hesitation. I slide in behind him. My arms hang free. I'm not sure what to do with my hands, what to grab on to.

"Hold on." Jay turns slightly so I can hear him above the engine. "Hold on to me."

I put my arms around him, lightly at first. When he picks up speed, I grip him tighter and my body slides in close to his. Interlocking pieces. I can feel, through my arms and legs, how strong his body is, how powerful.

Jay steers down the dark lanes, winding us back toward town. Houses flash by, car lights. And then we're on our own again, the only living things on the road to my house. Jay eases into the curves, gathering speed as he goes. I am holding fast. Even in the traveling wind I think I can smell sweat, cigarettes, leather. A shiver runs through me and then another.

When I feel the bike slow down, I almost want to cry. Somehow I thought that Jay would just keep going, riding through the night, riding those roads I've photographed straight into another world.

At the bottom of the hill I lean in and yell into his ear.

"You better let me off at the driveway. My dad."

It's not like my father cares anymore about my late nights. He's washed his hands of me. That's what he says when we're communicating. Washed his hands. But he doesn't like to have his precious sleep interrupted.

Jay gears down and makes a neat stop just off the road. My arms release, but I don't get off right away. I feel shaky, not sure I can stand. Jay laughs and turns toward me.

"I thought you were going to squeeze me to death. You weren't scared, were you? Haven't lost your nerve. You were always a brave little kid."

I feel my skin heating up again. With all this blushing I'm turning into somebody I don't recognize.

"No, I haven't lost my nerve." I slide off the bike, turn away slightly.

"Okay then." Jay takes the helmet and puts it in place. He leans in close and catches my eye. "Lu. I'll see you around."

He's gone before I can answer. I listen to the sound of the bike winding away, getting smaller. I turn and head up the dark driveway. The porch light is on, my father's one concession to the fact that he has a daughter somewhere out in the world.

Inside my room I strip off all my clothes and fall into bed. I lie flat and I can't help but see Jay's body pressing into mine. Instant reflex. Isn't that what I was thinking before? The body's need to be touched. And suddenly I want to be touched. All over. Every inch. Someone pressing me into existence.

Drifting into sleep I keep going back to those times with Danny and his crew on their bikes. Up and down the dusty hills, I'd be hanging on with all my might. Hanging on to Danny or to Jay—the same as a brother to me, back then. I remember how they were always real careful with me, Jay in particular. My father called him the wild one, but it was Jay who was always the gentlest, most thoughtful. Turning around before taking me on a run, giving me that smile and telling me not to be afraid. Telling me how he'd never do anything to hurt me.

2

Photographs. That's all I have of my mother since my father gave most of her things away. Black-and-white. Some color. There's the day she married my father at the courthouse in a plain white dress. Honeymoon pictures in Mexico, dark hair swept back and big silver earrings in her ears, looking exotic, not looking like she's from Rainey, Kentucky. Pictures with Danny as a little smiling boy, her body thrown around him like he was her own. And then there are pictures of me, a tiny wrinkly baby in her arms.

I guess that's why I picked up the old Nikon in the first place. I like the idea of making something real, something that will last.

As soon as my eyes open in the morning, I'm thinking about photographs, getting my body up and down into my basement darkroom. Even with my head pounding and my mouth dry as dirt.

Downstairs, my father is nowhere in sight. I'm sure he had important people to see at first light. Even on a Sunday. McClellan Means Sold. That's his motto. Real estate is his religion.

Lights on, I go through my gallery. It's a ritual before I start developing. I have to go through all the photos, stare at them, touch them. Bits and pieces of Kentucky. A sweep of highway. A curve of weeping willow. A straight line of tobacco.

Bits and pieces of my life too. Ginny in all her various personas. Danny playing his drums or stripped down and dirty, working construction. Close-ups of my gran Mac—her wrinkled hands, her tiny feet pressed into her old lady shoes. There's even a few of my father, his face and body tight and closed, looking at the camera like he's ready for a fight. And then there are the pieces of me. My eyes, my mouth, my brow with the ring through it.

Today I stop in front of the photo I took holding the camera next to my face in the mirror. Right after I had all the hair cut off. Until this year my hair was long, to the middle of my back. But I felt like it was weighting me down. Ginny took me to a cool place in Lexington. The woman asked me if I wanted to keep the hair after she cut it, but I didn't. They say hair grows after you die. Hair and fingernails.

And here's where I let myself think about the night before. Jay. The voice, the body, the gray eyes looking at me. The feel of him pushed against me. Maybe it was all a dream. A drug-induced hallucination. But in my new groupie-chick state I think I can still smell his scent on me. Sweat and cigarettes, leather. Studying myself in black-and-white, I have to wonder what Jay saw when he looked at me. He said I was all grown up, but what did he mean? Did he look at my hair, my clothes, my face, and wonder? Crazy Lu. Did he see a crazy little girl blushing at his attention?

I mix the developer and cut the lights. I like this part almost as much as when the faces appear on paper, like magic out of nothing. I like it because everything's by touch. Pitch black. Not even the darkroom light as a guide. My fingers know what to do without my eyes watching. Just the dark and my hands working at releasing the fragile strip of film from its canister, threading it so it runs smooth through a little wire maze. So much could go wrong at this stage. Tearing the negative, letting a little light in without meaning to. And once the developer is doing its stuff, you could misjudge and make the negatives too dark or too light—too thin or too thick, it's called. And then no matter how much magic you try to do, the picture will never be as good as you want it to be.

I check my glow-in-the-dark watch and wait. Usually I flip on the light at this point. But today I just sit, running through Jay in my mind, listening to my own self breathe.

When time is up, I flip on the light and release the negatives from their stew. Just right. Not too dark and not too light. I know I'm a good cook. I hang them up to dry on the clothesline. A strip of tiny Ginny faces, the scene at Huntsville, kids from school, a field of daffodils.

Coming out of the darkroom is like coming out of a cave, up from the underworld. Like Orpheus. Danny named the band because he loves that story. Orpheus went down under to find his lady, but he was warned not to look back at her or she'd be lost forever. And that's just what happened.

The phone is ringing when I get to the kitchen.

"Sorry about the scene," Ginny says right away.

"No problem. Hope it was worth it."

Ginny lets out a little sigh. "Oh man, this guy. He's really cute. I took him back to his dorm."

"A college boy, no less."

"Nothing happened, but he's going to call me today. We're going out next week."

"What about Taylor?"

"What about him? It's time to live a little. Anyway, you get home okay? Hope you didn't get stuck with Wade."

I'm about to tell her about Jay, but something stops me.

"Danny took me home."

"Cool. Gotta go. Mama's calling. See you to-morrow."

I grab my camera and head outside, walk slowly down the hill toward the lake. My father is proud of telling people that he bought this place a million years ago when lakefront property sold for a song. Now it's worth a lot. That's his thing, knowing the value of land.

I follow the curve of the lake and then head into the woods. The property stretches out for several acres—wild and untamed. Strange that my development-conscious father has left it that way. Nature to nature. My own primeval forest. I'm not in Rainey when I'm walking through the trees and brush. I'm not even in this century. I'm some-where in between worlds, in between time. I hold the camera to my face and focus on the way an old root knots and gnarls itself along the ground. I like taking nature, but only when it looks weird, twisted. Truth is stranger than fiction. Something I heard in an English class once. I couldn't think up some of the images I snap.

As I walk, it starts to rain. I can't feel it yet, through the thick growth, but I can hear it rustling the leaves overhead. I tuck my camera under my sweater and keep walking. The wet is bringing out all the woodsy smells—pine and moss. I'm almost to the edge of my father's property. There's a little cabin there. Danny's first construction. Built when he was going to UK at night, working for T&E Contractors during the day. Waiting for the music company to call, he used to say. He doesn't say that anymore. He has his own business now. He only plays gigs on the weekends.

Through the trees I hear voices. My father's. Someone else's. I creep quietly until I can see but can't be seen. My father has his back to me, arms waving out. His whole body moves when he talks. He is a large man, wide and powerful. His black hair began to go gray after my mother's death. It's mostly salt with a little pepper now. When my father moves to one side, I see that it's Jay he's talking to.

Truth is stranger than fiction. Jay is out of my

43

head and here in reality. He stands quiet and still, listening to my father until he's finished talking. Then he nods and says something back. The two shake hands—a good firm shake—and my father turns briskly away, heads back to his car. Jay watches my father leave, waves a hand in the air. He's just turning back to the cabin when I come out of hiding.

"Jeez, you scared me," Jay says, but he doesn't look scared. He doesn't look surprised at all. Like he knew I was standing there all along.

"What are you doing here?" I ask.

Jay shrugs his shoulder toward the cabin. "Your father's going to rent me Danny's old place for a while."

"I didn't know he wanted to rent it."

"Danny did some persuading."

"You didn't say anything last night."

"I didn't know if your dad would go for it. But he seemed okay." Jay points toward the bundle under my sweater. "Hey, what have you got hidden there?"

"My camera."

Jay gives a nod then raises his face up to look at the sky. "We're getting wet." His eyes find me again. "Want to come into my new place? Be my first visitor?"

"Sure."

The door is tight and swollen in its frame. Jay has to push at it. Inside is musty and dark. Danny left his furniture here when he moved. A table and some chairs. An old sofa. It's one main room with a small kitchen attached. I know the hallway leads back to the bedroom.

"No electric yet," Jay says. "I'll have to see about turning it on tomorrow."

The light coming through the windows is gray and soft. I walk along the edges of the cabin. Even with my damp skin I'm feeling hot. A fever. Maybe I'm sick. Maybe I caught something last night. I run my fingers over the surfaces. There's a layer of dust on everything.

"I'll have to give it a good clean," Jay says. He stands in front of me. "Can I see your camera?"

I take it out from under my sweater and give it over, watching him hold it with careful hands.

"I picked it up a few years ago," I tell him. "I've been fooling with it for a while. I have a darkroom in the basement—where you all used to practice."

"I'd like to see your photographs sometime," he says, and it's not like someone is patronizing me. I feel like Jay really wants to see my work.

"Yeah, okay." I shrug like it's no big deal.

Handing the camera back to me, our fingers touch. Jay doesn't pull back right away. His fingers feel rough along the tips. I know that's from playing guitar. But the rest of the hand is callused too. Without knowing what I'm doing, I take his hand and open it up. He lets me run a finger along the pads of his palm. They're tough and hard like Danny's.

"I've been working with my hands," Jay says in a quiet voice. "I did a lot of odd jobs out west."

We're standing by the window and the light is soft on Jay's skin. I let go of his hand and put the camera to my face. Jay's hand spreads out in a blur. I back up and focus and click.

Jay lets out a quiet laugh. "You haven't changed much," he says.

This takes me by surprise. I feel confused, almost hurt. "You don't think so?"

"I mean, you've grown up. You look different." I feel his eyes over me again. "But you were always watching things. Observant. You were always watching us when we were hanging out with Danny. A little elf. That's what I thought when you came out of the woods just now. You're like a woodland creature, a sprite."

I turn away, my skin rosing up again. It's true. I was always watching Danny and his friends. But now—an elf, a sprite? Once again I wonder if Jay thinks I'm a freak.

"I've got to go." My voice sounds funny in my own ears. Outside the window the rain has stopped.

"Come and visit anytime," Jay says, walking me to the door. "You know where I live."

I head down the road that leads to our house, one foot in front of the other. I wonder if Jay is watching me, but I don't look back. When I get to the bend and I know he can't see me, I start to run. I hold the camera against my chest so it can't bounce. I can feel my heart beating against the metal casing. Jay's hand there. A little piece of Jay inside my little black box. I'll have to take the whole roll before I can get to it. But I'm patient, usually. Patience is what makes a good photographer. Sometimes you have to wait forever for the right shot. When I get home, I head down down down, back into my cave, my underworld, right away. I stop at my face on the wall. Pointed chin. Big green eyes. I do look like an elf. Something from a fairy tale. But I'm not the golden princess like Ginny. Maybe I'm the witch or the bewitched or the fool.

3

Monday morning I hit the road in my old Chevy Nova. Dark green with rust spots. Not a sleek speed-ster like Ginny's cherry red Porsche. But it gets me where I'm going. Danny sold it to me cheap last year. I take the long way and buzz a little before I head to class. I have the routine down. A few hits and then plenty of air-out time. It's not that I care anymore. It's not like the entire faculty doesn't know I'm a stoner. But with only a few weeks to go I don't need a hassle. I just want to slide through.

Science, English, trig, horticulture. The morning floats by and then I'm free for the rest of the day. The so-called privileges of being a senior. My father thinks I'm a screw-up, but at least I didn't screw up enough to have to do afternoon sessions or summer school just to graduate.

In the parking lot I catch Ginny and Taylor in an intense powwow. I know better than to get involved, so I just give Ginny a distant wave and head out. These days I spend my afternoons at the Bide-a-Wee on the east side of town. It's the motel my gran Mac owns and still operates even though she's in her eighties. The last few months I've been helping out—after school and before I go to my real job at the Steakhouse. Mostly I think I'm here to keep Gran Mac company. It's not like my father spends a lot of his free time at the motel. He's always trying to get Gran to sell the place and move into one of those retirement communities. But Gran holds on, even with the motels on the bypass taking all of her business.

Some days I help Gran with the cleaning or I sit behind the desk and answer the phone when it happens to ring (about once a day). Mostly I talk to Gran Mac about her life before Bide-a-Wee, about my father before he met my mother, about Rainey before it became such a podunk town.

"Gran Mac, didn't you ever want to get away from here?"

It's the same question I always ask. We're sitting on the little porch in front of the office, the sun warming our faces.

"Why, Lulu." Gran Mac looks at me and blinks her sweet blue eyes open and shut. I wonder why Gran Mac's eyes are so sweet while my father's eyes are so hard. The way he looks at me sometimes, it's like he'd rather spit than call me his own.

"Where on earth would I *go*?" Gran Mac asks me back.

"Anywhere," I tell her, bringing up the camera. Gran Mac is one of my favorite subjects. Her snow white hair, the wrinkles cutting through her skin, the big blue eyes.

"This is my home," Gran Mac says, turning slightly and lifting her arm to take in all ten units of Bide-a-Wee.

Click goes the camera.

gran mac: home

Gran Mac leans in and puts her face right up to the lens. "This is your home too, Lulu."

I don't want to hurt Gran Mac's feelings, so I don't say anything back. For a couple of hours we sit, watching the cars pass. Gran Mac dozes on and off, pretending she's just resting her eyes. At three o'clock sharp she goes inside for some real nap time. This is what I'm really here for. To watch over the place while Gran takes her two-hour "catnaps."

I do some homework, listen to music on my Discman. Around four o'clock Danny shows up to check on a leak in number 9. I follow him to the room and sit on the bed while he works under the bathroom sink.

"Saw you at Landers'," I tell him.

"Yeah, I know. Jay said he ran into you."

I feel a tiny zap. Jay talking about me when I'm not around.

"You sounded good," I say.

"No shit. We're grooving again, with Jay back."

"What's he doing here anyway?" Trying to sound casual. "I thought he was long gone."

"Don't know. Guess he just got homesick."

I can't believe anyone would be homesick for Rainey, but I keep it quiet. Danny stands up and turns on the tap, checks his work. Satisfied, he comes and sits on the chair opposite the bed.

"What's up with you these days?" Danny's blue eyes are always smiling. "Haven't seen you in a while."

"Not much." I shrug. "Just getting by till graduation day."

Danny nods his head. "I know what you mean. I remember. It all goes by so fast."

"That's what people keep saying. But it doesn't. It doesn't now. While you're living it."

Danny laughs and runs a hand through his long blond hair. "I'm not going to argue with you. I'm not going to be one of those old guys telling you how it is."

"You're not old." I laugh, and I'm thinking of Jay. They're the same age. Ten years older than me. But it doesn't seem like such a huge difference. Not anymore.

"It's weird, Jay's staying in your old place," I say. "How'd you pull that one off? I mean, Jay was never one of Dad's favorite people."

"I know." Danny shrugs. "But it's hard for the old man to pass up a few extra bucks once a month."

"Ain't that the truth."

The light is hitting Danny just right, but I realize

I left the camera in the office. My fingers itch to focus and click. After a while Danny picks up his tool chest, and I follow him to his truck.

"Hey, we're playing Friday night. Mooney's. You should come if you want to. I could get you in if there's a problem."

"Mooney's doesn't card," I scoff.

Danny raises an eyebrow. "They don't, huh?" But he lets it go. He's not too old to remember what it's like.

The rest of the day drags on. I leave Gran Mac with her TV dinner and head for the Steakhouse. The job's okay. Ron, the manager, hassles me some-times about the hair and the ring, but I'm pretty good at serving people when we're in the weeds— crazy busy—so he can't get too wacked out. Good help is hard to find, after all, and I've been steady for two years—enough time to save up something for my ticket out of here.

It's after eleven o'clock when I finish wiping down my station. I'm too tired to change out of my white shirt and black pants so I have to keep the window rolled down all the way home. My clothes always smell like charred meat when I get done with a shift. I use up the rest of the joint from the morning, the smoke curling around inside and releasing me from the day.

Turning into the driveway, I catch sight of a light through the trees. I cut the engine and walk slowly down the road toward Danny's cabin. Jay's bike is parked near the porch. The lights are on inside and I can hear a trace of music.

It crosses my mind to walk right up to the window and look inside. A view into another world. It hits me that Jay is somebody I know but don't know. Old but new. I hear a noise and my heart speeds up. I rush into the shadows.

Silence again. Probably some little animal out in the dark, like me.

I turn and head back to the house. Once more I fall asleep thinking about Jay, wondering what he's doing at this very moment, only a stone's throw from my own bed. It's like some kind of addiction. Only two days and only a couple of quick hits. But already I feel a need. The way I crave the smoke day to day, the way I carry my camera with me, even in the dark.

4

For some reason when Ginny asks me what I'm doing Friday night, I tell her I'm laying low. It's not like Ginny and I tell each other every little thing. But it's new. This silence I'm maintaining about Jay. My own little obsession.

Is that what it is? So quickly? An obsession? The word makes me think of bad movies with crazed women going out of control. I don't think I'm out of control. Not yet. So far, what this amounts to is listening for Jay's motorcycle going down the drive, watching the light in his window from the edge of the yard, going on my own to see the band play at Mooney's.

Lexington is the closest big city. Another twenty-five miles past Huntsville. I wait to light up until I'm through all the known speed traps. It's not like I have a spotless record. I know what it is to have a cop light shining in your eyes, going through the usual questions and walking the straight line on the side of the road to prove you're sober. I've spent time in the Rainey police station waiting for my father to come through the door with that look of rage and resignation on his face. The warnings (out of respect for my father's position in the community) didn't make me curb my evil ways. They've only made me more careful.

The club is on the edge of town. A regular Orpheus gig. The bouncer vaguely remembers me as being with the band. The bartender gives me drinks without batting an eye.

Orpheus is already jamming, the guys cool and comfortable in the rhythm. Jill and Lena find me in the crowd. They wave me over to their booth in the back and squeeze me between them.

"This is the old wives' booth," Jill yells into one ear.

"They sound good, right?" Lena shouts into my other. "Jay makes all the difference."

I nod, sipping at my vodka and tonic, turning now to watch Jay. He's dressed in the same black jeans and black T-shirt. This time he has on mirrored sunglasses, as if the stage lights hurt his eyes. He's looking off to one side, nodding his head along with his chords.

Jill and Lena start pulling at my clothes, touching my hair and brow, dissecting my look. "Kids today." Jill shakes her head, but I can tell she's getting nostalgic. "Ah shit, man, we were wild too, back then. Not so long ago. What we used to wear . . ." Her words fade off in a jolt of reverb.

I look down at my thrift store finds. Black silky top with a stitched-in curlicue pattern. I know it's thin enough so you can just see my black bra underneath. The pants are boy pants, stiff, dark blue, some kind of shiny material. Sharkskin comes to mind. They fit perfectly. High-heeled boots from the sixties with little pointed toes. My hair is slicked back and my eyes are lined in blue.

Jill wraps her skinny bare arms around me. She's wearing a tank top with Orpheus in bloodred across the front. Her breath smells like gin.

"C'mon and dance with me." I can tell she's already on her way to sloppy. "Lena never wants to dance. Just 'cause I'm an old lady doesn't mean I can't dance."

I gulp down the rest of my drink and then I'm ready. We start on the edge, weaving to the music together. It's not like dancing with Ginny. Jill is funky but her moves are old, from another time. I remember that she's older than Dale, with a couple of kids from an early marriage.

I keep focused on the music, on making my body slide between the notes, but when Danny gives the mike to Jay for the new song, I feel Jay's voice pulling me up so I'm watching the stage. Vodka can make me fearless and so I keep staring even though I'm not sure if Jay is watching me behind his shades. The words—about longing and searching—make something start to ache inside. I'm almost relieved when Jay stops singing and the song slows to a close.

Danny grins at the audience, telling them the band is going to take a short break. Jill gets us more drinks from the bar and we head back to the booth. My hands are trembling just a little around the plastic cup.

Dale and Rob slide in beside their wives, giving me a nod. Danny has a groupie in tow. Big-chested and blond. When he sees me he wraps me in a sticky wet bear hug, and I catch the groupie's eyes icing over.

"This is my sister," Danny says when he lets me go. "Lu, this is Crystal."

Crystal gives me the up and down. I can tell she's not totally buying it since we look nothing alike. But she doesn't have to think about it for long because Danny pulls her off toward the back of the club, probably going out to the parking lot for some smoke.

I make small talk with Dale and Rob, trying not to notice if Jay is heading our way. Out of the corner of my eye I see him at the bar with Tom getting beers for the guys. Jay has his shades pushed back over his head and he's talking and smiling with a couple of women who seem to be hanging on his every word.

I feel something jolt through me, something I don't recognize. I think about Taylor's face as he watched Ginny walk away with another guy. Is this what jealousy feels like? I don't like it. I don't like this new thing taking over my mind and body. I start to stand up but Jay is blocking my way.

"Hey, leaving already?" Jay asks. His body brushes against mine, setting the beers on the table.

"Outside," I say. "I'm going outside. I need some air."

"Yeah, me too." And Jay is following me through the crowd, his hand on my back like he is guiding me even though I'm the one in front. Outside the cool air rushes into my lungs. After dancing the sweat is cold against my body. I start to shiver. We walk to the van and Jay unlocks the back and pulls something out. His leather jacket. He holds it out to me.

"I'm okay," I tell him.

"You're shivering," he says, and moves to hang the jacket on my shoulders. I let him wrap it around me, breathing in the smell. Leather and something else. Distinctly Jay. Behind the van I pull out my last joint and hold it up for Jay to see.

Jay's gray eyes are watching me. The color of the lake when it's cold. The color of the sky in winter.

"I remember when you were this big." Jay holds his hand down to his thigh.

"Time flies." I repeat the old phrase, lighting up and inhaling deep.

"Time flies." Jay laughs and keeps watching me.

I hold out the joint.

"I don't smoke much anymore," he says, but then his fingers brush mine. "But yeah, okay."

"How's the cabin?" I ask.

"Not bad." Jay talks with the smoke held inside. "I've gotten it cleaned up. The electricity on. You should stop by. It's pretty quiet way back there."

I wonder what he would say if he knew I watched him from the shadows. I wonder if he'd say I hadn't changed. Always watching.

When the joint comes back to me, I touch my lips against the damp end, where Jay's mouth has been.

"I like the song. The new song. You wrote it, right?" I look down at my shoes. The heels make me come to about Jay's shoulder.

"Thanks, yeah, it's mine. I've been working on a few more, but the band hasn't learned them yet."

"Were you in a band out west?"

Jay shakes his head, accepting the joint again. "I kind of left music behind for a while."

Cars come and go inside the parking lot. It doesn't feel strange being quiet with Jay. It feels old and comfortable.

"Hey, we better head back in," Jay says after a while.

I tap the joint out and follow him across the lot. At the door we run into Danny and Crystal. Danny's eyes are friendly, but knowing him so well I notice something different when he catches sight of us. Surprise mixed with something deeper. It takes a minute for him to flash his regular smile.

"Hey sis." He takes my arm and sniffs at the air

around me. "What are you doing out here?"

I shrug, feeling Jay's jacket heavy on my skin. I don't have time to answer; the noise is loud as we walk inside the club.

For the rest of the next set, I sit in the booth. I don't feel like dancing and Jill is too wobbly to push the issue. She begins to sway and suddenly she's grabbing on to me again.

"Outside," she whispers in my ear. "Sick."

I get her out and in between the cars before she starts to heave. I hold her head and wait. I've done this for Ginny so I know the drill. When it's all over I fish inside my bag for Kleenex. I try to lead her back to the club, but all she wants is to crawl up in the back of her car. I guess she'll sleep it off till Dale is finished. I make sure the doors are locked before I leave her.

Back inside, I go looking immediately for Jay. He's at the bar again, talking to one of the women he was talking to before. His gray eyes glance up. They hold me a moment and then go back to the woman's face.

A heartbreaker. Not just Danny. I know the score. Guys who rock have some kind of magic power. I know that Jay always had a reputation. A new girl every week. The wild one. My father's words from long ago.

At the booth I pull Jay's jacket off and leave it on the seat.

"Jill's in the car," I tell Dale, who looks unconcerned. He must be used to it. Lena waves and Danny stops me at the door.

"Hey, are you okay to drive? You could wait around and I'll take you home."

"No. I'm okay. Really."

He looks into my eyes. "Are you sure?"

"I'm sober, truly," I answer and I'm not stretching the truth. After the drinks and the smoke I'm strangely clear-headed.

Danny kisses my forehead and releases me. I'm gone before I can look toward the bar again. The road back to Rainey is slow and crowded with cars heading home from some big night, same as me.

Some big night. I have to laugh out loud at

myself in the dark. Did I think something was going to happen between me and Jay? My brother's friend. Somebody ten years older. Crazy Lu. I suddenly see myself as a little girl still waiting to grow up.

When I get home, I park the car and walk down the road. I stand where I've stood over the past week, watching Danny's cabin. Jay's cabin now. I know there won't be any light in the window. I know but I keep watching anyway. I can't help it.

5

"Look what the cat dragged in."

It's my father. Unusually present on a Saturday morning. Coffee and donuts on the table. The paper spread out around him. He is impeccably groomed. Starched white button-down and khakis. Even the pennies in his loafers are shined.

In my morning haze it takes me a second to realize there's someone sitting next to him. A woman who looks up at me, startled, with big brown eyes.

She is perfectly groomed as well. Soft brown hair pushed back with a plaid headband. Yellow shirt over crisp slacks.

I look down at my torn T and ripped jeans. My hair is sticking up from sleep. I didn't bother to take off my eyeliner last night, so I know my eyes are dark smudges.

"I wasn't expecting company," I say.

My father clicks his tongue—his subtle method of critique—and goes back to his paper. But he makes the formal introductions.

"Melanie—my daughter, Lulu."

"Good morning, Lulu," Melanie says in a bright, overly cheerful voice. I can tell she would rather be anywhere but here at this moment.

"Hey," I answer, letting myself stare. I know I can make people uncomfortable with that stare. It's something I've perfected with my father, with my teachers and the counselors at school. "I think we've met before."

"Yes, we have." Melanie smiles, jumping on it quickly. "At your father's office."

"You work there, right?" I ask, piecing it together.

"Well, yes." Melanie covers her mouth for a little nervous cough. "Yes, I do. For the past few months." She smiles again. It's a nervous habit, I realize. That smile. She is somebody who wants everything to always be okay. "I've only been in Rainey a little while. It's such a nice town."

I turn away, pour myself some coffee. I lean against the counter, sipping and watching, taking in the new. My father has never brought lady friends home before.

I can tell Melanie doesn't like quiet. She'd like to keep the conversation going, but she's not sure how. She looks back and forth between my father and me, keeping the smile on her face. I know I could leave them alone, ease her suffering, but I'm suddenly enjoying this.

"Your father tells me you'll be graduating soon." She takes the leap.

"That's right," I answer.

"Senior year—what an exciting time."

"Rah rah rah."

Melanie looks like she's been slapped. She's waiting for my father to come to the rescue but he's taking his typical stance. Absent behind the paper.

"So, what are your plans?" Melanie jumps in again. "I mean, after graduation?"

I shrug. "No plans."

My father grunts and finally snaps the paper closed. He squints at me like he's looking at me through fog. I'm not someone he recognizes anymore.

"Well, there are so many choices, at your age," Melanie says. My father turns to her and she keeps going, her voice less sure of itself. "I mean, with so many choices, it's difficult to decide. I know how it is." She looks back and forth from me to him. "I really do."

"Not many choices when you waste your time taking pictures all day," my father says, talking to Melanie, not to me. "It's not like she's on the honor roll. It's not like she has colleges knocking down the door."

"Hey," I wave my hand in the air. "I'm present, you know."

My father's eyes squint back at me. Silence. Melanie's smile is costing her something. She looks like she wants to fade into the woodwork. I decide to end her misery. I'm suddenly bored with the whole thing. I pour myself another cup of coffee and head for the basement.

"Catch you later," I call. "Thanks for the quality time."

"Nice to meet you, Lulu," Melanie chirps after me.

Before I'm totally gone I hear my father's voice. "See what I mean? I told you . . ."

"Well, Mike, when I was her age . . ."

I stop listening. I have no interest in what Melanie was like at my age. I'm sure she had the same sunny smile and nervous laugh. Trying to make everything sweet and meaningless in the world.

When I get downstairs, I don't stop at the wall. I go to the drawer where I've hoarded the old photo albums and flip to my mother. We have the same wide cheekbones and pointed chin and green eyes. The same dark hair. She wore hers parted in the middle and straight down the sides of her face, a thick veil around her head. In Mexico her skirts were short and her legs were thin and tan. She wore slip-on sandals on her small feet and silver rings on her thin fingers. She stood against old stone walls and at the top of Mayan pyramids, looking stately, like a Mayan goddess. In one dark photo she sits on a beach, her bikini revealing small breasts and a flat waist.

I run my hand along her belly. This is where I came from. This is where I lived before I was birthed into the world. When I cut the lights, it's like I'm going back inside the dark, into the womb. Quiet and comforting. Only a little glow from the darkroom light.

I mix the chemicals and pour them into their separate containers. Three magic potions. One for drawing the image out; one for stopping the image; one for fixing the image in place. When it's all ready,

I take a strip of tiny scenes and insert it into the enlarger frame. I work the enlarger up and down, making the first image big or small, cutting out what I don't like. The light flashes onto the photo paper for a few seconds and then I slide the blank sheet into the first container. Under the liquid, the image starts to come to life. Blurred white and then edges coming into sharper focus.

jay: working hands

Seeing the hands come to life before my eyes makes me feel young and stupid. I keep watching until the image goes past its prime, growing darker and darker under the ripples, until it's gone altogether. Fade to black. I pull the sheet out with my tongs and toss it wet into the garbage.

I take a deep breath, chemicals drawing into my lungs, and start again. This time I go with familiar subjects. Ginny, the bottle of Jack against her lips. Gran Mac, mouth open, eyes closed in one of her catnaps. More Kentucky roads leading off into the distance. Then, without meaning to, I'm working on Jay's hands again. This time I make them smaller inside the frame. I take my time with the shading, dodging part of the image, burning in the rest to make things sharper. The hands bloom into being, and I slide the paper into the stopper and then into the rinse.

Lights back on, I gently wash all the photos floating in a tub of water and then I hang them up to dry.

Jay's hands look ghostly, separated from his body. I think about the hand of God reaching down to Adam in that famous Michelangelo scene. I think about my mother's hands. I'm not sure I remember them, but they must have been soft, pushing back a strand of hair, brushing against my forehead, holding me close.

Suddenly I want to be out in the light again. Upstairs, my father and Melanie are long gone, the kitchen neat and tidy like they were never here. I walk out the side door and down the little hill to my mother's garden. I squat among the blooming iris and buttercups and tulips. It's like my mother's hands are still at work here, tilling the soil, lovingly caring for the flowers. But it's all an illusion. My father pays someone to keep the garden just like it was when she left it. Pretty sick when you think about it. A bad joke. I've had dreams where I come into her garden, all the flowers in bloom tricking me into thinking she's still here, alive. I go searching for her and the flowers suddenly start to grow bigger, shooting up and looming over me, gigantic faces peering down. I push through the colors, searching, calling her name. Suzanna, not "Mother" or "Mom." *Suzanna*. But I never find her. In the dream. I always wake up.

I'm still squatting when I hear a noise. A buzzing getting closer and then fading away again. Jay's bike, coming or going, I can't tell which. I make myself go back into the house and pull on some shoes and a jacket, head out again, this time for my car. I take off, heading toward Rounders. It's a bright clear day. I know I'll find Bunny sunning himself on the rocks.

The usual suspects are hanging out by the trickling water. Cattail Falls, this place is officially called. But everybody refers to it as Rounders. The air is thick with sweet smells. The Rainey cops know about this place but they never bother to raid it.

Bunny pats the seat beside him. He's never surprised to see one of his clients.

"You need something?" Bunny asks even though he already knows.

"Same stuff," I answer.

"No problem." He grins over at me and pats my knee. "But hang out for a while. What's your hurry?"

I lean back into the sun. "No hurry," I answer. No hurry today.

Alix and Darrell are there too. We pass around a joint and the sun starts to melt me into the rock. Bunny eases his hand onto my knee. I pull away and he laughs. Bunny's thing is patience.

We walk to his truck and make the exchange. A small stack of green for a bag of green.

"Hey." He leans in close. "I've still got some of that stuff I had last week. I'm telling you, you'll like it."

I can feel the net around me, Bunny reeling me

in, and for once I don't care. I hold out my hand, watch Bunny's easy smile as the pill slides down.

We head back to the warm rock. Everybody is quiet, watching the water. Nothing happens right away, but then I start to feel like I'm made of air, my body melting into the fading shadows. When I close my eyes, I see colors. My mother's garden. When I open them, everything is vividly clear. The light coming through the trees makes the waterfall holy. I listen to the sound of water trickling down. It is laughing, trying to tell me something. I keep listening, but the meaning fades away. Alix is talking to me and I nod my head, even though I don't understand her words either. I close my eyes and let it all float away.

It's dark when I feel hands against my skin, moving inside my shirt, rubbing at my breasts. I think I've been asleep but I'm not sure. I think of Jay's hands. Rough and warm. But these hands sliding over my body are cold and smooth. Snakey. I surface long enough to push them away.

"Hey, don't you want to party?" Bunny's voice

close in my ear, lips moving against my neck. "Come on, Lu."

It takes all my concentration to get myself up, off the ground.

"Shit," Bunny says, but he doesn't try to stop me. There are voices in the shadows, so I know we're not alone.

Somehow I make it back inside the Nova and find my keys. The road blurs and jumps under the headlights. Nothing looks familiar even though I know this is the way home. When I finally make the turn, the house is dark, the driveway empty. I stop the engine and open the door, but I can't make myself get out all the way. I don't know how long I'm there before I hear the familiar roar. The single headlight catches me full on.

"Lu?" Jay calls above the noise. When I don't answer, the engine cuts and Jay is there, squatting down in front of me. "Lu, are you okay?"

I nod but I can't find my voice for answering questions.

"Lu? What's going on?"

I try to stand up and Jay bends down to help me. I hold on to him and lay my head against his chest. He is warm and strong. I pull myself up, push my lips into his neck.

"Lu." Jay leans down to try to steady me and I press my lips into his. For a moment I feel it. He is kissing me back. Sweet and soft. Warm. Melting into colors. But then I am being held away. "Lulu. C'mon." His voice isn't angry, but he's serious now. "I think we need to get you inside."

I let him lead me into the house. He lays me gently on the couch.

"Are you going to be okay?"

I nod my head, watching him as if I am seeing him from a great distance, under water. Jay looks around, runs a hand through his hair. He crouches down and peers at me with his gray eyes.

"I better go. Your dad would freak to find me here, with you. Like this."

"He wouldn't care."

"Yeah, well, something tells me he wouldn't be too thrilled. We'd have some explaining to do." He hesitates. "Are you sure you're okay? Do you want me to call somebody? Danny?"

I shake my head and turn away toward the back of the couch.

"Nobody. Forget it. I'm fine."

My eyes close and the colors are still there behind my lids. Reds and purples. Yellows and greens. The flowers sprouting bigger and bigger, above my head. I search and search. But I can never find her.

6

Another Monday morning. Another week on the countdown. When I pull into the seniors' lot, Ginny is just getting out of her car. She's head-to-toe preppy. Paisley pink skirt and pink sweater top. Little tasseled shoes. Hanging with Ginny can be like hanging with some kind of southern belle Jekyll and Hyde. Split personalities. Sorority sister one day, black leather vixen the next.

"Lucinda." Ginny moves in close and I know

she's serious when she's using my real name. "I was trying to call you all last night. What's up with you?"

I shrug. "I was in the darkroom." It's a lie. I was out of it, under the covers, ignoring the world.

Ginny moves in close and puts her hand on my arm. Pink nails to match the rest. "There's something going around. About you and Bunny."

"Jeez, that took all of twenty-four hours." I pull away, not wanting to be touched by anybody, not even Ginny.

"What are you saying, Lu?" The blue eyes go wide.

I stare back at her. "What do you think I'm saying, Ginny? That I'm blowing Bunny for drugs?"

Ginny holds on to that for a few seconds and then her perfect face wrinkles up and she starts to laugh. One of the very cool things about Ginny, that laugh. Nothing fakey. Just all-out laughing.

It makes me laugh too.

"I don't even want that image inside my head," Ginny says.

"You and me both, sister."

"Well," Ginny breathes out. "It's not going to be easy for you today. I can tell you that."

"When is it ever easy?"

First period and I can already feel the buzz. A whisper here and a glance there. I tell myself I'm used to it. I didn't get to be Crazy Lu for nothing. Water off a duck's back. Only a few weeks to go and I'll find a place where nobody knows my name, my history, nobody gives a shit. Maybe out west instead of New York City. I wonder what the desert would look like through my lens.

But the morning drags on and the thought of getting lumped into Bunny's blow-job club is almost too much even for me to bear. When Wade comes up before my last class with that wide grin, I'm ready to lose it.

"You're breaking my heart, Lu," he says, putting a hand over his chest.

I slam the locker without saying a word and head out the door. It's been a while since I ditched school. I used to do it all the time. I probably hold the record for detention. I've been suspended but never expelled. Rainey doesn't like to go that far. Lots of father-teacher conferences. More counselors with letters behind their names. This year I'm such a good little girl, just trying to make it through. One unexplained absent hour this close to graduation won't sink me.

It's too early to go to Gran's, so I cruise down to the river. I park in the pull-off near the singing bridge and roll a thin one, just enough to calm the nerves. Bunny's stash. I weigh the plastic baggy in the palm of one hand. This is costing me more than the cash I paid for it, I'm thinking.

Inside the car, the sun is beating through the glass, making everything nice and toasty. I could curl up and go to sleep, but I grab the camera and head out along the water. Near the base of the bridge I start focusing. Graffiti all up and down the blue metal girders. It's called the singing bridge because cars going over the metal lacework roadway make a humming sound. Ten cars go singing by over my head. I count them as I click. The graffiti I'm framing is about love. Sloppy and exposed. Jason luvs Casey. Kevin and Tina 4-ever. Laronda n' Mitchell.

I hike up onto the road itself and frame the bridge head-on. The river is the dividing line between one county and the next. Depending on which way I'm heading when I leave, the bridge could be the last thing I see of Rainey. The portal to another life. This time when I think about leaving, I'm not seeing myself inside my green Nova, the backseat piled up with all my earthly possessions. I see myself on the back of Jay's bike, riding off into the sunset, nothing but the clothes on my body to remind me of home.

Back at Bide-a-Wee, inside my Monday routine, Gran Mac feeds my munchies.

"Oatmeal raisin, my favorite," I say as she sets the plate of cookies before me on the office counter. Gran Mac likes to believe I'm still a little girl and I go along. I try not to think about all the things I could tell her that might shock her heart to stopping. She knows about the problems. My father has complained to her over the years. But she seems to shield herself from reality, referring to my various troubles as "growing pains."

"Somebody's having a birthday soon." Gran Mac singsongs. "I'll have to get out my cake pans."

Gran's homemade chocolate cake. Another favorite.

"Will you be having a party?" Gran asks. I shake my head and she looks disappointed. I think about how sad it is that there are only two grand-kids for Gran Mac to dote on. And one very absent son. Gran Mac deserves a big family around her, adoring eyes, always welcoming her oatmeal raisin love.

"I remember my sweet sixteen party like it was yesterday," Gran says. Her blue eyes moist over, going the distance, almost seventy years. I don't bother to pick up the camera. I have this one already.

gran mac: sweet 16 memories

I've heard the descriptions so many times—the frothy dresses, the boys in suits, the daring first kiss—but I still can't imagine what life was like back then. When a kiss could mean something as binding as forever.

"Your grandfather was so handsome." A tinkling-bell laugh, a long sigh, then Gran comes back to the here and now. "Hard to believe you're already turning eighteen. By my eighteenth birthday I was engaged." Her blue eyes peer at me. "Is there anyone special?" she asks slyly. "A young man from school?"

I shake my head, choking a little on my cookie. What would Gran say if she knew about the Bunny buzz? If she knew about Wade trying to get into my pants just for bragging rights and nothing more? If she knew about my obsession with Jay. I can't imagine Gran's sweet sixteen memories inside my world.

"I'm not the heartbreaker you were, Gran," I tell her.

Gran reaches out to smooth down my hair. Her hand, fluttering a little, caresses my cheek. "You're such a pretty girl," she says. "My grown-up girl." Then she turns away and heads into her room for her catnap.

Gran has never said anything about my hair, my ring, my clothes. It's like she looks at me and only sees what she wants to see. My father looks at me and sees only what he wants me to be.

Ginny calls me to check in while I'm sitting at the desk. She knows about Wade, and me leaving early. She warns me to cool it or people will think the Bunny buzz is true.

"I don't really care," I tell her. "It won't matter when I leave this town."

I can hear Ginny pouting in the silence. Even though she knows my plans she still thinks we'll somehow be together. That I'll change my mind and sign up for UK at the last minute. That we'll get an apartment together.

"I hope you won't forget me when you're gone," Ginny says.

"How could I forget you?" I ask. "Besides, you'll come visit. Wherever I am."

This always soothes her and she settles down to tell me about Reid, the college boy. "I'm thinking about asking Reid to take me to the prom," she says.

"So, you're seeing this guy for real, now?" I ask. "What about Taylor?"

Ginny sighs. "Taylor can be such a little boy." Her voice lifts up. "Hey! I know how you feel about proms, but I wish you would come. The last big blowout."

"You've got to be kidding. Who would I go with? Wade or Bunny?"

"You could ask one of your brother's friends. Maybe that guy Jay."

I catch my breath. It's like sixth sense sometimes with Ginny. I wonder if I've done anything to give myself away.

"That would be weird. I mean he's ten years older."

"So?" Ginny asks. "He's pretty hot."

"Forget about it, Gin, proms are not my thing. You should know that by now."

"Okay, okay," Ginny cries.

The rest of my Monday, the rest of my week glide by. The buzzing comes and goes at school. I let it roll away in a cloud of smoke. I run into Bunny in the hall on Thursday and give him my famous stare. But Bunny is immune. His smile goes slithery.

"I know you'll be back for more," he says, and I can see he's talking about more than just the drugs.

Friday morning, my father surprises me again. He's waiting in the kitchen, a suitcase sitting on the floor.

"Going somewhere?" I ask, sliding on my shades. Best to have a barrier up this early in the day.

My father checks his watch. "You're moving slow this morning," he says, instead of answering my question. "You're still going to school, right? I haven't gotten any calls lately."

"No hooky, scout's honor," I answer, holding up my fingers.

A click of the tongue.

"Anyway," I press on. "I'm not the one with the bags packed."

Suddenly my father is not so cocky. He looks down at his well-manicured hands. He smooths a very smooth cuff.

"I'm going to a real estate convention in Atlanta. I thought I told you. I'll be gone for a few days. Danny is going to look in on you, so no monkey business." He hesitates and reaches out his hand as if he's going to take off my glasses, but I pull back. "I mean it, Lulu. Mrs. Quinn will be around too. She'll let me know if there are any wild parties, or such."

I let out a snort. "I'm sure she will." Mrs. Quinn is our very disapproving cleaning lady. Another person my father pays to keep things the way they were when my mother was alive.

"I'll be calling Danny to check in," my father continues, looking at his watch again.

"Is Melanie going too?" I ask.

My father's head jerks up. His eyes flash and for a moment it seems like he's at a loss for words.

"Yes," he answers finally. "Yes, she is."

Silence. We both watch each other. Dad with his squinting eyes and me behind my shades.

"Well then." He clears his throat. "I've left the number of the hotel in Atlanta. On the counter." He waves a hand in the air. "Just in case."

I shrug and my father turns away.

"Have fun," I call, but the door has already closed.

I sip my coffee and watch the clock. I could still make it to first period if I floor it all the way. But my father telling me to be good has the same old effect. That's my problem. I just have to do the opposite of what I'm told. Like Pavlov's dog, it's automatic. I know it's a character flaw. Like from some Greek tragedy we learned about last year in English. Maybe I am a tragic figure, doomed to always make the same mistakes. But I take off my shades and head down into my underworld. The darkroom is my school. I'm learning all I'll need to know.

When I surface again, it's dark outside to match the downstairs dark. Danny calls to see if there's anything I need.

"Do you have a gig tonight?" I ask. It's not like Jay has been gone from my mind, but I've kept him veiled. Dodging him out of the frame, like I do when I develop my photos. I can't think about the other night. The way I pushed myself, threw myself on him. I remember the feel, the taste of his lips, but I can't really remember if I just hallucinated his kissing me back for one quick moment.

"Not till next weekend," Danny answers. "We've got practice tonight. Trying to learn some new songs." Danny keeps talking but I zone out, remembering how I used to hang out at practice sessions when Danny was just starting up the band, years ago. That's before I turned the basement into my studio. It used to hold Danny's drum set and all the amps instead. I used to run up and down the stairs, bringing the guys Cokes and chips and sometimes beer. Listening to them make music and talk in between about girls and drugs and other things I didn't understand. "Hey, Lu," Danny calls across the wire. "You still there?"

"Yeah, sorry," I answer.

"I'm getting another call so I gotta go. Be good, okay? I mean it. I don't want the old man coming down on me for not keeping an eye on you."

"Don't worry. I'll be golden."

I head upstairs. Instead of going into my room I

walk down the hall. My father's bed is slightly rumpled, but the rest of the room is ultraclean. The double closets holding his crisp white shirts and his suits all in a row. Everything organized. I know it works at my father's nerves that he can't organize me as neatly. I'm sure it will be a relief when I'm gone, no longer his responsibility.

"I wipe my hands clean," he said once on the way back from a store downtown. That was in my shoplifting days. The urge so strong to just pick something up and slip it into my pocket, my bag. I could taste the adrenaline. That was before I started doing drugs. I guess I wanted the rush even then. I was pretty good, but I got caught twice. Both times security kept me in the little office in the back, calling my father and giving him the warning. People like to gossip but they don't like to see things in the papers. Everybody feels sorry for my father. After all, his wife died young and left him with this problem child.

I go to the bed and roll back. It's been so long since I've thought about my father having a particular scent. Now it catches me by surprise and takes me back in time. It wasn't always this way, right? The tension. The silence. The disapproval. I have this blurry memory of being held close, his face pressed against me. Some kind of spicy cologne and sand-paper, rough against my cheek, my forehead. My hair was damp when he pulled away. It must have been soon after my mother's funeral.

I roll into a ball in the middle of the bed and pull the pillow to my face and breathe deeply. It all comes back. The way I used to fit so snug inside his arms. But as soon as I started to get bigger, it all changed. The light in his eye. Growing dimmer, the way whites can fade to muddy gray if you're not careful when you fix your prints.

I jolt up in the pitch-black night, not sure where I am at first. Then I realize I must have fallen asleep, still in my father's bed. I pull the blankets around me and let myself slip back again. Not just my father's bed after all. Once my mother's too. Once I was small, cradled here. Between them.

7

I'm standing at my car when it happens. I knew I had to run into Jay sooner or later. Only so long I could keep him off the frame. He slows down and cuts the motor. He waits for me to come to him.

I take the plunge, but I make sure my shades are down.

"About the other night—"

"Forget it." His eyes are behind glass too, but his smile is the same old Jay smile. I feel something slipping off. Relief. I shift back and forth, looking off toward the trees.

"Where you headed?" I ask.

Jay follows my gaze. "Not sure. It's a good day. Just thought I'd keep driving. Haven't really had a chance to explore much since I've been back."

"Explore?" I ask. "What's there to explore? It's not like you didn't grow up around here, right?"

Jay turns back to me. "It's been a while. Things change."

The words hang between us. I feel my face flushing pink. Blushing never used to be a part of my anatomy.

"It's a great feeling," Jay continues. "Going down these old roads on the bike."

"I'd like to try it sometime."

Jay grins. "Want to come along?"

"Now?"

"Some other day if you're busy."

"I'm not busy." I shrug, act like it's no big deal. "Sure."

I reach into my car to get my bag with my camera and then, just like that, I'm wrapped around Jay, holding on while he shoots us out of town. The bike hums over the singing bridge just like in my daydreams. I let the fantasy take hold: leaving town with Jay, not looking back.

The wind whips at my face and clothes as Jay picks up speed. The light falling through the trees splashes across the road. Jay turns us onto smaller and smaller roads. The world flashes by—shacks and barns and cows and small, ragged children waving to us from the side of the road. I never want to stop this motion, the bike making my whole body tremble slightly.

Late in the day, Jay does stop. When I swing off the bike, my legs are wobbly beneath me. We buy some food and drinks in an old country store and sit along the road at a picnic table. People keep staring at us out their truck windows. I look down, trying to see what they are seeing, and I like the way we look together. Both in black with our shades on and our short hair matted down against our skulls. I wish I could take a picture of the two of us, but I settle for framing Jay inside my lens. He doesn't cheese it like so many people do when they suddenly feel the camera pointed their way.

"When are you going to show me your photographs?" he asks.

"Anytime," I answer, thinking how few outsiders have seen my gallery. Ginny of course, and Danny. I've shown Gran Mac some things, but she's never been into the darkroom. My father never sets foot in my world.

Back on the bike, Jay heads us up and up a winding hill. At the top he pulls off the road and cuts the engine. He waits for me to slip off and then without a word we start walking through the trees, up a path. We keep going until we're looking out over a crop of cliffs, the green land rolling gentle toward the sky, pink as the sun goes down.

"This is one of my favorite places," Jay says. "You can almost see Rainey." He points off to the right.

"Why did you come back?" I ask suddenly.

Jay thinks before he answers. "Sometimes you don't know you'll miss a place until you're gone."

I stay quiet. I can't imagine missing anything about Rainey. Except Danny and Ginny. And now Jay.

It's easy standing quiet without any words between us. All day I've felt this comfort. No need for extra conversation. And now I become aware of how we're standing, side by side so our arms are almost touching. I want to pull him toward me. I want to feel what it's like to have him wrapped around me the way I've been wrapped around him all day on the bike.

And then it happens. Jay is turning toward me, leaning down. Our lips touch, and it's like falling, melting. No drugs inside my veins now, just a kind of drowning, sinking.

Jay pulls back just a little. His eyes—the gray seems darker now—looking deep into me. I don't look away. I want him to see that I'm ready. I'm ready for this.

We head back down the hill in silence. Back on the bike, we fit together. The dark rushes at us, the night flowing through us. It seems to take forever until we are humming over the singing bridge again. Jay slows down for the last few miles, keeping to the speed limit, then he makes the final turn and stops in front of my door. We both wait. I'm not sure what to do.

"Do you want to come in? Dad's gone for the week." I see Jay think this over. "You could look at my photographs."

That settles it. Jay nods and turns off the bike. I like the way it feels to have him follow me, up the stairs and into the house. Down into my cave. I flip the lights and stand back, nervous now. What will he think?

He takes his time going through my gallery, looking at each photo carefully before moving on to the next. He nods his head thoughtfully.

"These are really good, Lu," he says, and I feel this glow of warmth. Nobody, not even Danny, has taken so much time. "These are amazing. Did you learn this stuff in school?"

"No way," I scoff, the idea of Rainey having classes like photography beyond the realm of possibility. "I just kind of picked it up. From books and stuff."

"Amazing," Jay says again. He turns to look at me. "Is this what you're going to do when you leave here?"

"It's what I want to do," I answer. "Dad doesn't see much point in it, but this is what I want to do. Take pictures."

"Don't stop," Jay says. "It's easy to get talked out of following your dream."

I nod my head like I know what he's talking

about. Maybe I do. I remember Danny talking less and less about music after college, listening to my father more and more as he droned on about the need to have a foundation, build something real. My father helped Danny get started on his own construction business.

Jay moves toward the clothesline of newly dried photographs. I realize the one of his hands is still hanging up to dry. I want to hide it but it's too late. The flesh and blood is reaching out for the paper image.

"You make ordinary things look new, different," he says after studying the photo for a while. "That's a gift."

He turns toward me and his hand is reaching out, touching my neck, my face. Again he is watching, his eyes searching, looking for something. I keep my own eyes open and locked. I want him to know. I'm not the little girl who used to follow him around. Not anymore.

Jay sighs, runs a hand through his hair, shakes his head as if trying to clear his brain.

"I think we need to take this slow," he says.

My skin feels tight against my bones. Every part of me is opening up, pressing outward. I want to tell him how little time there is left. A few weeks and I'll be gone. I want to tell him, but I don't.

I follow him back up the stairs and into the night. I watch as he gets back on his bike. I want to throw myself into him, feel his lips on me again. But I'm not desperate. Am I? I'm not desperate enough to throw myself where I'm not wanted. I am a little girl again, suddenly. Little Lu. What do I know about anything? Maybe Jay is just humoring me. Doesn't want to hurt my feelings. I turn around and I think he calls my name but I keep walking into the house. All I want now is to hide in a hole, lose myself in the dark.

8

"Sundays suck, you know?" Ginny takes a cigarette from the stash by her bed and lights it. "Sundays make me crazy."

We're sitting in her palatial suite on the top floor of her family's mansion. Her mama would die to know she's smoking in her pristine digs, but her parents are at the country club for Sunday supper. The Cavanaugh house has been in *Southern Living* a couple of times. Ginny can't move a stick of furniture without her mama having a cow. It's like Ginny doesn't really live here. She has to move in between the family heirlooms. She has to sleep neatly in between the perfect matching sheets.

"At least we're fully loaded," she says, leading me down to the family's well-stocked bar. In Kentucky Sunday usually means no booze because it's against the law to sell it. But at Ginny's house there's always an open bottle. What blows me away is that her parents never check the stock like my father would do. The bottles get lower and Mr. Cavanaugh just sends out for more.

Ginny hands me a beer and pours herself a neat glass of Jack. She flips on the gigantic screen TV but is more interested in telling me about premed Reid.

"A doctor. You'll make your mama very happy," I

tell her, waiting for her laugh.

"I wouldn't mind being a doctor's wife," she says quietly. "A couple of kids. We could raise them here." She looks at me. "You think that's dumb, right?"

"No, it's okay." I get the words out, but I know Ginny can tell I'm lying. I can't imagine a worse fate than being tied down in Rainey for good.

"Loner Lu," Ginny says, and now the laugh comes, loud and sharp. She downs her whiskey. "Let's hit the road."

We are silent until the LEAVING RAINEY sign looms in the fading light.

"Ginny, are you going to let me in on where we're going?" I ask.

"Johnny Angel's is open on Sundays," she replies with a wicked grin.

"But it's a school night." Immediately I feel like some kind of goody two-shoes.

"Who's checking us in?" Ginny asks.

"Not a soul." I know her parents won't come home from the country club till late and my house is still empty.

"We're not dressed." I look down at the jeans and old shirt I threw on.

"We look great," Ginny pronounces. "We always do." Her face in the fading light is glowing. Even when we're just hanging out, she carefully applies her makeup. My face is bare.

"I must look about ten years old," I say, thinking about Jay. Cradle robbing. Maybe that's what flashed through his mind, stopped him from going any further.

Ginny keeps one hand on the wheel, but reaches for her bag with the other.

"Here, work some magic," she says, holding out her makeup kit.

With the car making its fast curves, I put on some foundation, shadow, mascara, lipstick. It almost feels like I am putting on Ginny's face and, not for the first time in the many years we've been friends, I think about what it would be like to be in Ginny's shoes. Her wealth and popularity and easy-going spirit. I wonder what it would be like to have a mother, a distant one, but a mother just the same.

Somebody who cares about how you look, what face you present to the world.

"Spring fever," Ginny says. "That's why I'm feeling so weird." She keeps sipping at the silver flask she snagged from her daddy. She is whipping us faster and faster along the snaky road.

After Dead Man, I close my eyes, going back to yesterday, Jay's body snug against mine when he took the curves. I feel the car speed up so I know Ginny must be trying to pass a junker, but then she lets out a kind of gasp and my eyes are flying open to headlights flashing straight ahead. Ginny jerks the wheel back to one side and the car zigzags over blacktop. I want to close my eyes but I can't and then Ginny is in control again, the steering wheel gripped like steel under her hands.

My heart is pounding loud inside my head. Neither of us says anything for a long time. I watch the trees and signs go by, slower now. As soon as she can, Ginny turns off the road and brings the car to a stop. She sits without moving or talking, barely breathing, staring straight ahead.

"That was close," she whispers finally. A frightened little girl voice I don't recognize. Then there's a pause, and suddenly her laughter is tumbling out like always. She bows her head over the steering wheel, the weight of her laughter pulling her down.

Something bubbles out of me—I'd say it was giggles, though I'm not the giggling kind. Is this what happens when you look death in the eye and survive? Giggling. I can't stop and we both just sit helpless with laughter. Finally, Ginny wipes the tears that have been streaming down her face and takes a good long swig of Jack.

"Actually, that wasn't so bad," she says matter-of-factly. "It's just it caught me by surprise is all."

I nod, wanting to play along, kidding ourselves that we didn't just almost meet a car head-on. We know the statistics. Every year there are at least a couple of kids in the graduating class. Funerals, articles in the paper about the need to keep kids in Rainey. Nothing ever changes.

Ginny gets us back on the road and slowly

brings us up to speed. I keep glancing at her out of the corner of my eye. Her fingers are wrapped tight around the steering wheel and there's a determined look on her face. I know she must be shaken up but it's like she's willing herself to not be scared. In the club parking lot she doesn't say no when I pass her the joint. She inhales deeply and holds the smoke in for a long time.

"Let's roll," she says, and we pass by the bouncer without a hitch. Inside there's a decent crowd moving to the beat the DJ is making. Ginny pulls me along to the center. She keeps hold of my wrist, dancing close to me for a while as if she needs my strength. When the music starts to really surge, she lets go, spinning away.

I watch her, the lights making her blond hair glimmer, a golden thing in the dark club. A flame. She is like a flame burning brightly. It's strange that she's the one who wants to stay in Kentucky, thinking about a husband and kids already, and I'm the one who wants to leave as fast as I can. I wish I had some of Ginny's fire; suddenly, I wish I had some of her heat. A fireball rushing out and away, leaving nothing but ash in my wake.

9

There are other photographs of my mother. Ones from when she was a little girl. School mug shots and blurry home pictures with scrawly writing on the back. Some color, but mostly black-and-white.

Suzanna with kittens

Suzanna and the neighbor boy

Suzanna and Ray—daddy's little girl

My mother was an orphan when she married my father. Her daddy—Ray—was a truck driver. He died when she was about sixteen, when the truck he was driving jackknifed on a highway somewhere farther down south. Her mother died from cancer just a few months before Suzanna met the man she was going to marry. I don't know how I know these things. I just do. I think she must have told them to me, even when I was so little. I think she wanted me to know why it was just her. That's the way it felt. Just me and her. My father was always in the background. Danny was there, of course. But he was a different kind of presence because he was older.

When I hold the photographs close I can see it. The way we look alike. Thick dark brown hair and big green eyes. But she was prettier. I look at her kid face and I don't see the hardness I have. There's just one high school shot and she's so neat and clean and smiling. Sometimes in the mirror I try to imitate the look. Serene. Placid. But I can't. Except maybe when I'm high, floating.

I'm high and floating now, one joint gone and working in the dark. I guess I'm the most serene standing over my magic potions. The photos from Saturday. More highways and old shacks. Farmers looking startled by the side of the road. Jay leaning back against an old fence. Jay sitting on his bike, watching me.

There are lines on his face. Something I didn't notice before. But in the close-ups I see the crow's feet around his eyes. The lines shooting from his mouth when he smiles. I run my hands down my own cheeks. My face has no lines. It's soft and smooth. I know that time gives people lines. Time and hard living. I think about the small things Jay said on our Saturday trip about being out west. It wasn't always easy, he said. Odd jobs here and there. Nobody knowing you, the way they do in Rainey.

"That's just what I want," I told him.

"That's what I wanted too. At first."

And that's all he said about it. He went quiet, the lines on his forehead getting deeper for a while.

I want to ask him about the desert. I want to ask him if he'll take me there. But all I can do is listen to the buzzing of his bike going down the driveway. All week, the sound is there at sunup and there again after dark. I know he's working some job with Danny. I listen to the sound and I touch myself.

Let's take this slow.

His words.

I want his hands, slow, running down my body.

I know I've never felt this way before. This want. This need.

Always searching and never finding.

His words again. The song he brought back from his time away. I want him to find what he's looking for. In me.

10

This time when Ginny asks about my Friday night I let her in on the gig. Orpheus is playing at the old VFW just outside town. The show promises to be full of drunken rednecks and hometown losers, but Ginny wants to tag along anyway. The college boy doctor is home visiting his family, so Ginny's at loose ends.

"What about Taylor?" I ask, and Ginny shrugs. She steers us toward Huntsville first for a refill on the usual poisons and then we're pulling into the VFW parking lot. We sit for a while and I share the bottle, let the whiskey burn through me. I'm thinking how you have to fight fire with fire. All week, it's like a fever is burning up my skin.

I haven't seen Jay face-to-face since the kiss. Once we make it inside the club, I watch him from the shadows. His eyes are shadeless. The gray looks pale, almost white in the glaring stage lights. The room is hot, sweltering. Danny's chest is bare and Jay is wearing an old-fashioned sleeveless white undershirt. His shoulders are broad and the muscles along his arms are hard and cut. He is not a large man, but you can see the power in his body. You can feel it in the bass line.

When I step into the crowd to dance with Ginny, his eyes find me. I know it without checking. I will myself not to look up. I know that if I look at him it will show. The week of listening in the dark. Whispering his name.

"Somebody's showing some interest," Ginny says, nodding toward the stage.

"What do you mean?" I ask, breathless.

"That guy. Jay. He's watching you."

Still I don't look up.

"Maybe he's looking at you."

"I don't think so." Ginny pulls in close. "Have you been keeping secrets?"

I shake my head. A flash of guilt. I *am* keeping secrets. But then what is there to tell? One kiss. Two. Silly schoolgirl fantasies.

Ginny keeps looking back and forth between us, but I concentrate on the music. The band is sounding better and better. All the lines coming together in an easy groove.

When the set ends, we duck outside for some cool air and a few more hits of Jack. We lean back on the hood of Ginny's car and watch the sky. It's full of stars. Ginny checks her watch.

"It's almost midnight, birthday girl," she says. "I want to give you this." She takes my wrist and loops something around it, clicks it closed.

I look down at the string of tiny silver beads with the single heart charm. Something she always wears.

"Ginny—"

"I want you to have it."

"But Gin—"

She grabs my wrist above the bracelet and squeezes.

"I want you to have it." And the words are final. She's drunk, but not too drunk to give away her family heirlooms without thinking about it. I finger the little beads as Ginny sips at the bottle. Her eyes are bright when she looks at me.

"You're my best friend, you know," she says.

"I know."

Silently we pass the bottle back and forth. The parking lot is full of people, hitting their own private stashes. Laughter and catcalls. Trucks revving up and squealing out. Ginny heads back in to find the bathroom, but I stay outside awhile longer, feeling the dark and all the voices around me.

"Lu."

And I know it was his voice I was waiting for. Jay is standing before me in the full moonlight.

"It's my birthday" is all I can think to say.

"Danny told me." He seems to hesitate, but then he moves in and reaches to push some damp strands of hair from my forehead. He is the old Jay, protective, looking after me as a little girl. But in an instant he is the new Jay, pulling me close. I know he can taste the whiskey on my lips. I wonder if he can feel the fire.

"We've got one more set," he says, but he doesn't let me go right away. He holds me tight against his body, pressing his mouth into my hair.

"I'll wait," I tell him. And I do, dancing with Ginny in the crowd, sitting with Jill and Lena at the wives' table. It doesn't matter what I'm doing. Our eyes keep finding each other. Even with the stage light glare. I think Ginny is the only one in the whole room who could know, but she stops asking questions.

When Danny announces it's time to say good night, Ginny smiles and leaves without asking how I'll get home. I wait for the guys to pack up. Danny jumps down from the stage and pulls me close and tells me happy birthday.

"I'll see you tomorrow night, right?" he asks, and I nod. Gran Mac's fixing me a birthday dinner. "Will the old man be there?"

I shake my head. My father called this afternoon. Said he's extending his trip another week. Shocking that he's abandoning ship so close to the end—my final days in the house. Not so shocking, he didn't say a word about my birthday. Out of sight, out of mind.

Danny must think I have my car, so he doesn't ask how I'm getting home. He gets caught up in a mini fan club of smiling ladies, and so I slip outside and wait beside Jay's bike. After a while Jay comes out the door and loads his bass into Danny's van, and then he is starting the bike. We don't say a word as I slip on back. It's totally familiar now, wrapping myself around Jay. I hold on tight, down the highway and around the curves.

"What about your dad?" he asks when we slow down in the driveway.

"Still gone," I answer.

In front of the cabin he stops the bike. My knees are wobbly again, just like Saturday, as I follow Jay inside. I stay near the door, not sure what to do. Jay reaches into a drawer.

"This is for you." He hands me something in a brown paper bag. It's a book of old black-and-white photographs. Walker Evans. "I like his work. It kind of reminds me of your stuff."

Jay leans over my shoulder as I flip through the images—men and women staring out from history, thin and dirty, but strong; landscapes so sad and abandoned. I can't get the words out to thank him. All I can do is lean back, into his body. I feel a resistance at first, the same hesitation from before. I set the book down and turn. I press my mouth onto his. I want to imprint myself onto his being so he won't be able to push me away.

But he doesn't even try. The kisses are like candy. A sweetness. A hunger. I can't get enough. I am opening up. Every inch filling up with Jay until we are sharing the same breath, the same heart-beat. Hours, maybe years, pass and we are on his bed, lying side by side in the dark. Everything by touch. I begin to pull at my clothes. I want to know what it's like. Skin against bare skin. But his hands steady me. His fingers work carefully at the buttons of my shirt and my jeans, his mouth kissing the places that have been revealed, finally releasing me, pale and new and waiting.

I hold my hands against my chest, suddenly shy. Unsure what to do next.

Jay stops immediately. His fingers caress my face and he looks into my eyes. I am shaking just a little. I can't find my voice but I nod my head.

Yes. This is what I want. Yes.

He takes my hands and gently moves them down, onto his body. I close my eyes. Everything by touch. Fragile and smooth. Magic. A sharp pain. My breath catches in my throat and then a warmth rippling, building. All at once I am hot and cold and I can't get close enough. To Jay. I can't get my body close enough. Skin upon skin. Fire and ice. Every inch of me trembling inside this new sensation. I want to cry out but I put my mouth onto Jay's neck, biting down. I want to merge our blood, become one inside this heat spreading out, flooding out in waves. An ocean of fire and blood, crashing inside me.

And then there is quiet. Jay lets me down gently

against the pillow. He says my name and wraps his arms around me. I curl up against him, afraid to pull away, afraid he won't be there if I let go. Our breathing slows, separating out again. Two different rhythms. I blink my eyes open and closed. I can see the moon through the window. A full moon, watching us with her pale moon face, bathing us in her light. I feel changed. Holy. I feel like my skin has been peeled away so that everything I touch hurts.

11

I don't know if I sleep. I must go to sleep because when my eyes open again, there is more light inside the room, but it seems like I am in a semi-wakeful state all night, listening to Jay's breathing, feeling his body pressed into mine.

Without moving him I pull myself out of his sleep grip. My body feels shivery as I walk into the other room, like my bones have been transformed into something softer, more pliable. I find my bag on the couch and pull out my camera. Back in the bedroom, I survey the scene. Our clothes are lying across the floor, near the bed, as if our bodies are still inside. It looks like a murder scene, the clothes marking the places of the dead. I focus and click.

discarded things: end of innocence

Then I lean over the bed and focus. There is blood on the bottom sheet. Just a little patch, like a small red heart. And there is Jay. Lying on his stomach now, his face turned to one side on the pillow, an arm reaching out as if to find me. Inside the frame his face is content in sleep, his full lips slightly open. I know what those lips feel like against my body. I know how hot his breath feels against my skin.

jay: first love

So cliché, but there it is. My first time, my first love. The word is, I will remember this always. And I believe that I will. It seems impossible to forget this newness, this fire.

As I'm clicking, Jay opens his eyes. He blinks a

few times, staring at the lens, then his lips curve up, laughing. He reaches out and I put the camera aside.

"Lu," he whispers close to my ear, and then again, "Lu." I can't say his name. I can't speak at all. It's all new again, our bodies joined together, our breathing slow and steady and then speeding up. I keep my eyes open, watching his body hovering over me. I run my hands over the veins along his neck, throbbing like they do when he's singing. It seems to me he is singing now, his voice pitched so only I can hear.

And I am singing too, silently, singing out, radiating song and light. When it's quiet again I can still hear it, the sound of loving, can still feel the rhythm of pleasure in my blood.

Jay kisses my eyes and then he leaves me. I watch his body as he moves across the room, pulls on his old faded jeans. I've known the body for a long time, on the surface. But now I know its secrets, the hollowed-out places, the tenderness, the strength.

Alone I wrap the sheets around me like a shroud. It does feel like I've gone to another realm. Somewhere peaceful and calm. It doesn't seem possible that I could open the door and find myself still within the Rainey town limits.

After a while the smell of coffee brings me out of bed. I rummage through the murder scene on the floor and pull on my jeans. There's a sweater on a chair and I pull that on too. Jay's scent against my body. So quickly, I've become used to it.

In the bathroom I stare at my face in the mirror. My eyes are wide and green and I am smiling. I think I look like a mischievous cat who has swallowed something she shouldn't. A canary. I splash my face with water, run a hand through my hair.

In the kitchen Jay kisses me as he hands me a mug of coffee.

"Did you sleep okay?" he asks.

"I don't know," I answer. "I think so."

Jay doesn't smile. He becomes serious suddenly. He touches a hand to my cheek. "I thought we were going to take this slow," he says, and I think I hear regret and it squeezes at my heart. "You know I would never do anything to hurt you, Lu."

Words from long ago. I nod my head. "I know. You don't have to worry about me. I'm a big girl now."

Jay drops his hand and turns to pour himself some more coffee. "How long will your dad be gone?" he asks.

"Another week. But don't worry about him. He hardly notices what I do anymore. He doesn't care."

"I think he'd care about this." Jay turns back, but he's not looking at me. He's looking down at the coffee in his cup.

I shrug. "I'm eighteen now. I can do what I like."

"And Danny. He might flip out."

"It won't be an issue. You're friends," I say, but I remember the look in the Mooney's parking lot and suddenly I'm not so sure how Danny will react. But I push it aside. "I've got this birthday thing tonight. Gran Mac's cooking dinner. I want you to come."

"I don't know," Jay says. "It might be weird with Danny. We'll see."

I turn away slightly. I want to close up my ears, shake off reality. Too soon for it to be intruding on this new world. Jay makes me breakfast, a perfect omelet.

"Fry cook. That's one of the odd jobs I did in Arizona. An old run-down diner in the middle of nowhere," Jay tells me while we eat.

"What's it like out there?" I want to know. "It's desert, right? All flat and sandy?"

Jay nods. "Miles and miles of nothing. But the way the light hits the sand at a certain time of day, it's like nowhere else."

"I'd like to see it. I'd like to photograph the desert. Maybe you could take me there." I hold my breath and wait.

Jay looks away, then back. His eyes find me and it's like he's studying me. Then the smile opens up. The old smile that makes me smile back.

"Maybe," he says, still smiling, and I feel all warm inside. My plans falling into place.

After breakfast a steady rain sets in, beating against the windows. It keeps us inside all day, making the rest of the universe seem more and more unreal. For now I don't want to leave the little cabin in the woods. I sleep and wake to more caressing, Jay's body wrapped around me, pressing into me.

When I wake again, it's late afternoon. I hear Jay's acoustic guitar, fingers searching for the right notes, the right sequence. No words, just music. I stand in the doorway and watch him, lightly strumming at the chords, stopping every once in a while to write something down on a piece of paper on the coffee table. The rain has stopped. He puts down the guitar and we walk out into the dripping world. Everything is wet and new. We make our way down to the lake. The sun is low in the sky, lighting up the water. Jay holds me and we rock gently with the motion of the waves lapping up against the shore. It seems strange to me that the lake is still here, that everything is still here, outside the cabin, outside Jay's arms.

12

"It's the birthday girl!" Gran Mac opens the door wide and I am smothered in her warm kisses and rose water scent. She lets go and her blue eyes blink up at Jay.

"And who is this young man?" she asks.

"You remember Jay Shepard? Danny's friend from high school."

"Of course," Gran answers, reaching out to take his hand and pat it.

"He's staying in Danny's old place. I thought he might want to come along."

"The more the merrier." Gran smiles, leading us through her small kitchen into the living room. Danny is already there. He pops up from the couch and I get another big hug. Then he looks past me to Jay. I'm not sure if I'm imagining it but his smile freezes just a bit.

"Hey man," he says, and his voice sounds confused.

"I ran into Jay and he wasn't doing anything so I asked him to come along." The lie is already there, and I feel my heart speeding up. It's easy for me to lie to my father, but it's weird to start doing it to Danny. Danny's face seems to relax. He has no reason to think I'd lie to him. He turns to find his new lady friend. Teresa. I recognize her from the VFW. Tall with long dark hair and a nice smile.

"Danny's told me a lot about you," Teresa says, and she seems sincere, not like some of the other groupie chicks Danny brings around.

Gran Mac has fixed an enormous feast, all her specialties. Fried chicken and garlic mashed potatoes; corn pudding and new spring peas. Danny has brought two bottles of champagne and we drink them both with dinner. Even Gran lets her glass be filled again. She begins to giggle like a young girl.

"I don't mind a little champagne now and then," she keeps saying.

I hand Danny my camera to take a picture of the two of us. She is all white—white lacy blouse and white skirt. I am in one of her dresses from long ago, a black crepe de chine with rhinestone buttons going down the front. My hair is slicked back and I'm wearing dangly earrings and Ginny's silver bracelet. The pointy high heels on my feet make me feel older.

"You're all grown up," Gran says after the picture is snapped. She takes my chin between her fingers and studies my face. I feel my cheeks flushing hot. I wonder if she can see it, the change since yesterday. Loss of innocence. Jay tattooed on my skin. She giggles and lets go of me. "I wish your father could have been here."

I nod my head out of politeness, but I can't really say I miss his presence.

Teresa goes into the kitchen to help Gran with the dishes. Danny pulls me against him on the couch.

"The years, they start to fly by," Danny says, nodding toward Jay sitting across the room, watching us. "Isn't that right, man?"

Jay nods back. "The truth," he says softly.

"Yesterday Lu was just a little thing, following us around. Remember, Jay?"

And again Jay nods his head. "I remember." He keeps his eyes on Danny now, not glancing at me. Something is passing between them, but I'm not sure what. I pull away a little to look up at Danny. He's smiling, but his face is tight.

"Time. I don't know where it goes," he says. "So many things change."

"Here we go again. The old man talk." I want to lighten it up.

Danny laughs. "I do feel old these days. It seems like just last week, Jay and I, we were in high school."

"Getting nostalgic for the good old days?" I ask.

"Not really," Danny answers. "I wouldn't want to go back. But sometimes I wish things had gone a different way."

I keep watching his face, his eyes. It's the first time I think I've seen regret. But it's gone in an instant. Gran Mac is coming back through the door with the birthday cake. Teresa flips the lights and the candles make Gran's face glow as she sings the birthday song. I blow out the flames and Gran brings out the presents—a new lens from Danny, something I'd told him I wanted. A pair of tiny diamond earrings from Gran. She will have given me all her jewelry before she dies. That's what she tells me sometimes.

We hang around a little while longer, but then Gran starts to look tired and that's our cue to leave. I hug Gran and thank her for all the trouble.

"No trouble at all. Not for my sweet girl," she answers.

I want to laugh at that, but I don't. Tonight I do feel sweet. Full of cake and champagne and love. New love that takes my breath away when I think about it. Snapshots inside my head. Images from last night, this morning, today.

Out in the parking lot, Danny follows us to the bike. "Heading home?" he asks, and I nod my head, maybe too quickly.

"I'm beat," I tell him. "I was out late watching you all play."

Danny grasps Jay's hand in a tight shake. "Take it easy," he says. "That's my little Lu, you know."

Again I feel something passing between them.

"I know," Jay says. He gets on the bike and starts it up. Danny keeps watching us as I swing on back. I put my hands lightly around Jay's middle, not wanting Danny to see how familiar I am, how easily my hands reach for Jay. I think I feel Danny watching us all the way down the road. The sweetness begins to melt away and I feel confused, a flash of anger. Jay is Danny's oldest friend. I don't see how things could shift so fast.

Back at the dark house, Jay slows the bike down and it's like a question. My answer is to hold on tight and so Jay takes us on to the cabin. Inside he keeps his distance, glancing at me with cloudy, faraway eyes. I know he's thinking about Danny. But neither of us say anything about it. I take out my pouch and roll a joint. Jay doesn't refuse when I hold it out to him.

The smoke does its job, elevating me to a different level. It doesn't matter. Danny's disapproval.

Nothing matters outside this place.

I look up to see Jay running one hand over the neck of the guitar.

"Play me something. Play me what you're working on."

Jay shrugs. "It's not much." But he picks up the guitar and begins to work out the chords again. "No words yet," he says. "I've just been hearing this in my head since I've been back." I watch his hands moving over the strings and I feel it again. A heat blooming under the skin. I know what it's like now. To be gently played by those hands. Rough and callused from the chords, from the construction work he does every day.

I slide off the couch until I am kneeling on the floor between his knees. I place my hands gently on the body of the guitar, feel the sound inside the wood. He slides the guitar to one side and I am leaning into him, feeling his heart beating inside his chest. I think it is beating just as fast as mine. I want to press our hearts together, but he is holding back, his fingers wrapped tight around my arms.

"Lu." Just a whisper. "Little Lu."

"Not so little anymore. You said it yourself."

I feel the strength, holding me away. I push against it. I am just as powerful. I know it in my bones.

"You're going to show me the desert." A statement of fact. Not a question.

Jay keeps his eyes on me, searching.

"Is this what you want?" he asks finally. "Is this what you want, Lu?"

"Yes," I tell him, and again, "yes."

Slowly, slowly, he releases his grip and his hands lie motionless at his sides. Carefully I undo the buttons on his shirt and then work at the top part of my dress, unhooking the rhinestones and pulling the fabric back over my shoulders. I rise up and wrap myself around him. Now I can feel it. Our hearts rushing together. The rhythm takes us out of ourselves. This is no longer my body, his body. Together we are lost inside this motion, this rocking of love.

13

Days go by and it's like I'm moving back and forth between times, between worlds. I do my usual routine: school, Gran Mac, the Steakhouse. But nights I stay with Jay.

My body is new to me, precious. I see the way it is changing. It's like something being polished, honed to perfection. Blooming into life. I can feel the blood pulsing through my veins, the nerve endings zapping out signals. Every inch of me miraculously alive.

I am sure that Ginny will notice when I run into her between classes. I don't see how anyone could miss the before and after. But she seems preoccupied all week, quick scattered conversations before she rushes off to one place or another. She doesn't even ask me about the VFW, what she saw happening with Jay.

When Saturday morning rolls around again, it seems so natural, waking up in Jay's arms. We spend hours touching and talking. After lunch I ask Jay to teach me how to ride.

He steers the bike out into the driveway and holds it while I get comfortable. It's a big machine, but not too big. My feet reach the blacktop. I can keep it steady between my knees.

Jay points to the lever near my left toe. "That's the gear shift," he says. "You've got to find neutral first, and that's a little tricky because you have to click all the way down—click, click—and finally do a tiny little up click."

I keep trying it until finally I feel the rhythm.

"You know you're in neutral if you kick start and the bike stays in one place," he says.

After a couple of chokes the bike roars to life.

"Good, that's neutral," he yells over the noise. He shows me how to give it gas, a little at a time.

When we're purring in neutral, we go through the gears again. I'm used to a stick in the old Nova, but it's different on a bike. If you let the clutch out too hard you can pop a wheelie or kill the engine. After a while I start to get the tapping down into first and clicking through the gears beyond, but I'm exhausted.

"That's enough for today," Jay says. "You keep at it, it becomes more natural."

I cut the engine and Jay places a hand on my thigh before I swing my leg over.

"Always watch the muffler," he says. "Don't burn yourself. Muffler burns never heal."

I nod my head. I know this already. More words from long ago. I can't remember now if it was Jay or Danny warning me.

We take a break for food and then we head off again, Jay speeding us out of Rainey. We go west, driving through the knobs—the little hills that roll along the Kentucky landscape. Soon we're deep in Mennonite country. We pass by the black horse-drawn buggies, whole families dressed in formal black and white, from another era. The children peer out at us, but the older folk don't seem to notice us at all.

Jay winds us toward a small lake he knows about, hidden deep inside some hills. The sun is hot today—almost like summer. As soon as we're hidden from the road we take off our clothes and jump in.

The water is cold, a jolt running through me. But it makes me feel alive, tingly.

Out in the sun again, we let ourselves bake naked on some rocks. We pass a joint back and forth and the smoke gets me talking.

"Crazy Lu, that's what people call me in school." I turn toward him. "Do you think I'm crazy?"

Jay watches my face. "No crazier than most of us."

"But there are things—" My words stop. I want to tell him things that maybe he doesn't know because he's been gone. I'm stripped naked before him—not just my body but my soul. I want him to know. "I used to have to go to all these counselors. I never talked to them. Not the way they wanted me to. It makes me so angry. Just thinking about those guys sitting there, waiting for me to spill my guts. As if that could change anything."

I stop talking. I feel something choking up inside. It's like I want to cry and it shocks me. I never cry.

Jay wraps me in his arms. Our bodies are so warm from the sun.

"It's okay, Lu. It's okay to be angry as long as you don't get wrapped up in it. It's good to talk about stuff, get the anger out. Otherwise it can destroy you, make you bitter."

My father's face flashes in front of my eyes. The photograph I took of him once. I called his name and came around the corner and snapped. Candid camera. When I developed the image, I was blown away by the anger. His first reaction to my voice. Anger.

"My father is a bitter old man," I say. "I don't know what he wanted to do. When he was young. I don't think it was real estate. All his life. Real estate."

"Maybe you should ask him sometime."

I shake my head. "I can't imagine having a conversation like that." One on one. Heart to heart. I put my hand over Jay's heart. I can feel it beating slow and steady.

"Sometimes it takes some distance," Jay says. "You have to get some distance to see things clearly."

"Distance is the plan."

Jay nods but doesn't say anything. I pull away a little and watch him. Up close the lines on his face are like tiny rivers. I run my fingers along his crow's feet. I want to know about life. I want everything to happen at once.

After a while Jay begins to dress and I follow his lead. Soon we're buzzing back to Rainey. When we turn into the driveway, I feel a jolt.

"Speak of the devil," I say, although I know Jay can't hear me over the roar of the engine.

My father is pulling his bag out of the trunk of his car. He turns to look at the sound and it's just like the photo. Instant irritation. He shades his eyes against the sun to make the double check. His daughter on the back of Jay Shepard's bike.

Jay slows to a stop and cuts the engine. I swing off to face the music.

"You're back," I say.

My father nods, watching Jay. I see the suspicion in his eyes, and even though it's true, it makes me sick.

"Jay gave me a ride into town. The Nova's been acting up."

The lies roll smooth off my tongue. My father nods again and then turns away from us, takes his bag into the house.

I glance toward Jay. "I'll come by later," I tell him. He looks back and forth between me and the house and then nods, heads off down the drive.

Inside the kitchen, my father is looking through the fridge.

"I hope you haven't gotten into any trouble," he says with his back to me.

"Nice to see you too," I reply, watching as he prowls around the kitchen, presumably looking for some sign of my badness. "Did you and *Melanie* have a nice time?"

He winces when I say her name. "It was a productive conference." He comes to a standstill in front of the sliding glass doors, surveying his domain—the deck and lawn down to the lake. Then he reaches into his briefcase on the kitchen table and pulls something out.

"I picked this up," he says without looking at me. "Happy birthday."

I'm surprised that he remembered after all, but it's not like he took a lot of time with the choosing. It's a T-shirt, with ATLANTA written in bold letters. Probably something he picked up in the hotel gift shop.

"Thanks," I manage before turning my back. "I'm going downstairs. I'll catch you later."

He seems disappointed that I'm not more grateful for his small token. I leave it on the kitchen table and head down into my cave. I stand in the dark for a while, breathing in the chemical fumes, steadying myself for work. I need to erase my father from my head.

When I'm clear, I realize I haven't been down here all week. The images of Jay have been piling up, rolled tight inside their tiny canisters. I pull them out and wind them into the metal cage, wait for the chemical to caress the negatives.

As soon as they're cooked, I hang them up and go carefully down the tiny screens. There are the

141

clothes lying on the floor; Jay's face against the pillow; the rosebud of blood. I feel the heat rising. I want to go back to this moment, throw myself on the bed, start the whole thing over again. The ache of the new.

Today I don't have the patience to wait for the negatives to dry. I take out the blow dryer I keep on hand and set it to cool, gently blowing at the string of frames and cutting them into strips. I start with Jay's sleeping face, so peaceful as it appears under the developing liquid. And next, his eyes opening to me.

I spend the rest of the day looking at Jay on paper. When I come upstairs, it's dark. I can hear my father watching TV in his bedroom. I doubt he'll emerge again till morning. I glide through the sliding doors and follow the moonless road to the cabin. Jay's bike isn't there. I feel something heavy. A weight bringing me down. Everything has happened so fast, I haven't had time to think jealousy thoughts again. But they hit me full force now. I wonder where Jay could be, away from me. I think about the women who watch him when he plays. Am I any different than they are? I watch him, mesmerized, as he stands inside the spotlight.

For a long time I wait outside the cabin, thinking about the similarities. A wigged-out fan waiting beside the stage door. The night is cool and I am cold, shivering. Back inside my own room, on my own bed, I close my eyes and go through all that's happened over the past week. With my father gone it's like my body grew wings and went soaring above everyday concerns. Now I know there will be a shift down, gearing into neutral. I'll have to play it cool even though cool is not how I feel. I think about the sun baking our stripped-down bodies this afternoon. I feel my whole being burning with desire. I run my hands along my breasts, down to my thighs. An instrument to be played. I tell myself I'm waiting for sleep, but deep inside I know I'm waiting for the sound of Jay's bike.

When I hear it the clock is already reading two A.M. I wrap some clothes around me and retrace my steps.

Light and music. I hear the same song Jay has been working on. The melody coming out stronger now. I press my hands flat against the screen door. Jay looks up and I think about the first time I came to him out of the woods. A woodland creature, a sprite, he called me. I feel like something unearthly now. I want to reel him in with my power. Bewitch him as I am bewitched.

"Lu. You're always catching me by surprise."

But I don't think anything I do surprises him. Not really.

He opens the door and I wrap myself around him. A spell, a charm. I taste whiskey on his lips and cigarettes.

"Where have you been?" The words are out before I can stop them.

"I didn't think I'd see you tonight. Your dad—"

"It doesn't matter."

"We should take it easy."

My thoughts from before but hearing them out loud pushes a button, fuels the fire.

"He can't stop me."

In the bedroom in the dark my hands know just what to do now. My lips brush along Jay's neck where the blood rushes in a fierce pulse. I close my eyes and see the desert. Everything hot and wind-swept. Radiating light and heat. Fire. Jay's touch searing through me. The deepest burn. I never want these scars to heal.

14

All week I keep sneaking out to be with Jay, coming back before dawn, the house quiet and still. One morning at school Ginny catches me in between classes.

"I'm getting worried about you," she says. "You're becoming way too solitary."

"Look who's talking."

Ginny shrugs and grins. "Reid's been keeping me busy."

I want to tell her about Jay, but I can't put it into words yet, this new thing glowing inside. I don't want to try. Maybe I'll show her the photographs sometime soon. Photographs saying things I can't speak out loud.

Saturday night Orpheus has another gig at Mooney's. Inside the club the ladies are in the same booth. It's like I've stepped into a *Twilight Zone* except that I know I'm different. When I watch Jay up on the stage, I know he is watching me back, the secrets of the dark hanging between us. During the break, Jay sits beside me and finds my leg under the table. He keeps making small talk with Danny and the guys, but his hand is running along my thigh.

After the set he follows me home. We pull off beside the singing bridge and duck in between the trees. Pressed down against the seat, I close my eyes, but I'm seeing the names written in spray paint, the messages of love. I suddenly want to write our names somewhere, see them side by side. I want Jay to write his name on me, deeper than spray paint, something that will never wash off. Lu + Jay = Forever.

"Tell me what you thought. When you first saw me." Whispering it in the dark when we're quiet and still. The only sound—the hum of cars flashing by on the road above us.

Jay's fingers are playing along my ribs, strumming out the melody that won't leave him alone.

"Somehow I knew. I knew this might happen."

"What do you mean?"

Jay lets out a sigh and his fingers go still. "This is going to sound crazy, but you were one of the things I thought about sometimes while I was away."

A flutter in my rib cage. I hold my breath.

"Not all the time," Jay continues. "But when I was thinking about home, I'd remember all the things I missed and I'd remember Danny's little Lu, trying to tag along with us on the bikes, to gigs. I remembered you as a little wild thing, fearless."

Not so fearless, not anymore, I'm thinking. So many little fears plaguing me now. Passion, love, whatever this is that I'm feeling with Jay, it opens you up. This is what I'm starting to understand. It

147

opens you up to pain, jealousy, ugly feelings. Even tonight, sitting in the booth listening to the band, I couldn't stop noticing how other women were watching Jay.

"I want you to come with me," I say. "When I leave here. I want us to go together."

Jay lets out another sigh and pulls up, begins to button his shirt. "You've got your whole life ahead of you, Lu," he says.

"I've got some money saved." I keep going. "I'm leaving here after graduation. Nobody knows. Not even Danny. I was thinking about going to New York, taking some photography classes, but now I'm thinking about going out west, like you did. We could go together, on the bike. I could take pictures. We could get odd jobs here and there. I'm a good waitress, believe it or not."

Jay reaches down and his hand brushes my cheek. His eyes look wet in the dark. "We'll see, Lu," he says softly, and then he looks around. "It's late. You better get home before your dad sends the cops looking for you."

"I've told you before, he doesn't care."

"I think he cares more than you know."

Jay kisses me and leaves me behind the wheel. I start the car and wait till I hear the sound of the bike's engine revving up. Once more he follows me. I keep glancing back at the single headlight in the rearview. An eye keeping watch over me, making sure I get home.

15

Sunday I know Jay is busy with family obligations and band practice. I stay in the darkroom all day, working on the photos again. I want Jay here with me in my laboratory, watching the experiments come to life. I've never felt this way before. Never wanted anyone to meddle in my work. Photography has always seemed like a solitary choice, which has suited me just fine. But now I want to share it with Jay, this sense of wonder, making things happen with my own hands.

When I come up late in the day, I smell food cooking. Melanie is in the kitchen, wearing a perky yellow apron.

"There you are, Lulu." She smiles her bright, nervous smile. "We were just going to call down to you. We thought it would be nice if we all had Sunday dinner together."

I glance from her shining face to my father, sitting in the living room, hidden behind the newspaper.

"Would you mind setting the table, Lulu?" Melanie asks. "I don't know where everything is."

I shrug myself out of my shock and start opening cabinets, setting plates and silverware on the table. I can't remember the last time my father and I sat down to a Sunday dinner together.

And Melanie has gone all out. Roast beef and baked potatoes, stewed tomatoes. My father eats silently, nodding now and then at something Melanie says. I watch the two of them without saying a word. I realize Melanie is older than I'd originally thought. Maybe early forties. There are a few strands of gray in her blond hair and I can see she wears concealer under her eyes.

"How many weeks now till graduation?" she asks.

Funny. I have to think about it. Wrapped up in Jay I haven't been counting the hours like I did before. "Three," I answer.

"Will you be going to the prom?"

Here we go again. Why is everybody so fixated on proms? "Proms aren't really my thing."

My father grunts.

"Oh, but you should go," Melanie breathes. "It's something you'll never forget. I remember my senior prom like it was yesterday."

"Do you remember your senior prom like it was yesterday?" I ask, turning to my father. He watches me for a minute with narrowed eyes. I know his first wife was his high school sweetheart and she got pregnant senior year. That's why they had to get married. She took off when Danny was five.

"You *are* going to graduate, right?" My father takes the offensive. "I mean, I won't be supporting you while you repeat classes next year?"

"Never fear," I answer. "I'll be off your back soon enough."

It seems like he is about to say something, but he thinks better of it with Melanie around. I guess he wants to keep a little charm around her. I wonder what Melanie sees in him. A beauty and the beast attraction. My father isn't bad looking for an older guy, but he has beastlike qualities.

We go silent and I can see Melanie struggling. I can tell she's somebody who needs small talk like a junkie needs a fix. She keeps putting things forth, trying to roll us into a real conversation. But both my father and I have perfected the one-syllable dialogue. Finally she resorts to the monologue: her life before Rainey. Born and raised in a small town in Tennessee. Worked as a secretary mostly, but wanted to try something else. Finally got the courage to leave one small town for another, Rainey being a huge leap in terms of population and opportunities.

"I'd always wanted to try real estate," she says. "But I just never had the courage until I met Mike." She turns her smiling face to my father and I follow her gaze. I'm shocked to see that he's watching her and there's something there. His eyes aren't quite so harsh. His face has softened. A feeling leaps up inside me. Jealousy again? I'm too disoriented to answer when Melanie turns to me and asks if I want dessert.

"No," I stammer, pushing away from the table. "I've got homework to do."

"Homework." My father's eyes go hard again. "Will wonders never cease?"

I ignore him. "Thanks for dinner," I say to Melanie.

"You're welcome, Lulu," she says, blinking up at me. I can tell she's disappointed. She was probably envisioning some girl one-on-one while we did the dishes together.

I head upstairs, and truly do some catch-up for school tomorrow. A few sonnets for English, a handful of problems for trig. I'm closing my books when I hear the stairs creaking. Even on the wall-to-wall carpeting I can tell it's two sets of footsteps heading down the hall to my father's room.

Twelve years. It's not like I think my father has

been a monk, but he's never brought anyone home to keep overnight. I jump up and pace the room, head down the hall. I don't want to be so close to my father's new life.

At the cabin Jay's bike isn't there, but this time I know the door will be open. I sit back on the couch and reach into my bag, roll a joint. I keep thinking Jay will appear before I finish the whole thing, but I'm down to a pinch of ash before I know it.

I lie back and close my eyes. The smoke fills my head, spinning me off until I'm dreaming of my mother's flowers, the blue sky overhead. Jay is there and we are making love inside the garden, the petals falling down around us, covering us in softness and sweet fragrance. But then a sound begins to pierce through everything, a loud, persistent wailing. I put my hands over my ears, but Jay keeps pulling them away.

Listen, he says. *You have to hear it.*

The sound gets louder and louder and the sky gets brighter and brighter until I am sure I will go deaf and blind. I call out her name. Once, twice. And then I feel hands on my skin, gently caressing me,

154

my mother's hands, but when I look up it is my father, staring down at me with his hard eyes.

"Lu?" It's Jay's eyes now, close, watching me come out of sleep.

"I was dreaming" is all I can say.

Jay leans down and kisses me softly. "Practice went overtime and then I was out with the guys. Maybe you should go home. It's late."

I nod as Jay pulls me up from the couch. My head is still full of my mother's garden. Jay brushes his lips along my neck before I head down the road. Inside the house I listen for voices, for any sound at all. But all I hear is the TV going in my father's room. I stand at the end of the hallway for a long time, listening.

16

The middle of the week turns slow for Jay. Danny's company is in between jobs. A couple of afternoons I check to make sure Gran Mac's okay, leave the car at Bide-a-Wee, and head out with Jay into the country. We continue the driving lessons and the tours into the parts of my homeland I've never seen. My camera fills up with more images of small roads and run-down houses and old faces.

Late on the second day the rain catches us. A sudden thunderstorm. The water drives against us, soaking our clothes through in seconds. We are on an empty stretch and it takes Jay a little while to find some shelter. An old barn not far from the road, the doors thrown open.

Inside is dark and warm. There is a pile of hay in one corner. We take off our clothes and wring them out, lie down in the softness. The rain overhead beats out a steady rhythm.

I start thinking about how Jay has not said yes or no to my proposition.

I want you to come with me.

The words are there between us.

"What were you dreaming about the other night, when I came home?" he asks instead. "You were saying something. A name."

Suzanna.

I feel his arms around me. I know I can tell him anything.

"Suzanna."

There is a pause. "That was your mother's name."

I pull away. I can't help it.

"I know it must have been hard," Jay says in a soft voice. "Losing your mother so fast, so young."

"We all have something." Words I've heard someone else use. Maybe a counselor. Maybe the one who liked to look on the bright side of everything. Every cloud has a silver lining.

"But it must have been scary. You were there."

"I don't remember it. Not really." I close my eyes. Red and purple, yellow and green. And blue. The colors are there behind my lids.

"It's amazing what the brain can do. Hide things. Tuck them away." Jay stops. He seems to be choosing his words carefully. "Sometimes you have to work at remembering so you can move on."

I think about the techniques I use in the dark-room. Dodging, masking light. I think about my father. "My dad doesn't work at remembering. He gave away all her stuff right after it happened."

"Sometimes it's easier that way."

The rain has stopped. I can hear a trace of thunder, rolling soft, already miles away. We dress in silence.

On the way back home, Jay takes it slow. The roads are slick and dark from the rain, steam rising up in places. I think about what Jay said. The brain dodging out images, scenes it would rather not replay. I see my father's large hands held up, covering his eyes.

See no evil.

I've always thought he looked at me and saw only what he wanted me to be. But now I wonder. Does he ever really look at me at all?

17

Saturday I head over to Bide-a-Wee. Gran is having her hair done, a once-a-month affair. So I'm watching the counter for the afternoon. I keep expecting to hear Jay's bike pull up to keep me company, but it's Danny who appears out of the blue.

"I have some time today," he says, glancing around. "Anything need fixing?"

"Not that I can tell." But I follow Danny through the little strip of rooms, checking the toilets and the sinks for leaks. When we get back to the office, Danny's eyes keep moving around as if there's something he's misplaced.

"The old man came to talk to me," he says finally. "Says he's seen you on the bike a couple of times with Jay."

I feel something sparking inside me. "Once. He saw me once on the bike. Jay was giving me a ride home." White heat. That's what it feels like. Piercing my flesh. "What right does he have?" I want to know. "To spy on me?"

"He's your father, Lu." Danny's blue eyes keep flitting on me and moving off again. He doesn't like being the messenger, but something is bothering him. I can see it now. He's taking sides. "Maybe you should think about it, Lu. Whatever's going on. With Jay."

"What do you mean, 'think about it'?"

Danny shrugs, pushes the hair out of his eyes. "It's just . . . I know Jay. I've known him for a long time."

"He's your friend."

Danny lets out a deep sigh. "Yeah, he's my friend. So I know a lot about him." Slowing down, choosing the words carefully. "He's maybe not the best influence, if you know what I mean."

"No, Danny, I don't know what you mean."

"He's been around, Lu. Okay? He's ten years older than you and he's been around."

I let it sink in and the white heat just keeps intensifying. "That's kind of like the pot calling the kettle black, wouldn't you say?"

Danny blinks a few times, as if nobody's ever

called him on his lady-killer ways.

"But I'm not going after my best friend's little sister."

There. It's out in the opening. The suspicions. Cradle robbing.

"I'm not a little thing following you around anymore. Or haven't you noticed?" Danny starts to say something, but I cut him off. "And Jay's not 'going after' me. I'm old enough to know what I want. Besides, I won't be around too much longer, so you don't have to worry about all those bad influences. You won't have to worry about me at all."

Danny stares at me. "What are you talking about?"

"I'm taking off. After graduation."

"Where?"

"I don't know. Maybe out west."

"Is Jay going with you?"

I want to say yes, but I don't want to make a fool of myself. If Jay denies it. So I just look sideways. Silence making it seem like a confirmation.

Danny keeps staring at me. Through the white

heat I can feel something piercing my heart. Danny and I have always been so close. But there's never been any test. Danny has always taken my side until now. He's always been so laid back. Never showed any similarity to my father. But now I see he's judging Jay. Just like all the other losers in this small town. Wild Jay. Crazy Lu. Labels. Small town labels. The only way to drop the label is to drop the town, fast.

"Maybe you've been here too long, Danny." I say it and I know I'm cutting to the quick. I see the flash of pain in his eyes. But I can't stop myself. Blind rage. Residual anger from feelings of abandonment. I'm being abandoned now. "Maybe you've been in this small town too long. You've got small town ideas."

I breeze past Danny, outside and into my car. I know Danny will stick around till Gran gets home. He'll feel that obligation. I head the car toward the bypass, not sure where I'm going. At the shopping center I pull in and find a pay phone, dial Jay's number. No answer, so I try Ginny, ready to tell all. But her mom says she's out for the day.

I stand watching the cars go in and out. Same

old Saturday afternoon ritual in a dead town. Rainey folk checking out their sad little shopping center. I can't imagine being stuck in this same routine my whole life. I don't see how Danny takes it. I don't see how Jay wanted to come back. Suddenly I see myself as Jay's salvation. Maybe he was just out of gas. Needed a kick start to get going again. I see us going and going and going. The speed of light. Across the desert. Across the whole country.

I get back into the car and drive. Going in circles. Circles around Rainey. Faster and faster. I'm like one of those spinning tops you play with when you're a kid. You wind it up just to let it go, and the top spins off, faster and faster. But it never really goes anywhere.

18

Camerahead. The only way I can get back to a calm place at the end of the day is to put my face behind the lens. Look at the world blurry and then focused. One piece at a time. The road curving past the singing bridge. The small towns outside of Rainey. The view from the LEAVING RAINEY sign. The sun going down over a long empty field.

When I'm tired of my own scenes, I flip through the pages of the book Jay gave me. It says that Walker Evans believed the camera was a tool, like a paintbrush or a pen. He wanted the images to speak for themselves—facts, not interpretations.

I stand in front of my gallery wall looking at the facts of my world. Me and Ginny, growing up. Small town kids, getting wasted, nothing else to do. Gran Mac, happy in her old lady routine, never even thinking about leaving her home. My father's constant anger. My brother's easygoing love. My lover's hands, waiting to touch me.

My life doesn't seem complicated in black and white. Easy to follow. Easy to understand. No room for feeling tangled up and twisted. No room for outside interpretation. Facts. Boxed in, separated out, contained.

19

I don't tell Jay about my conversation with Danny, but I know something's up between them. Jay comes back from practice on Saturday night quiet and removed. He works at the song, but it's still stuck. No words. When we reach for each other in the dark, it's like we're drowning, holding on for dear life. Every breath is precious. Air being sucked in and out through the same pair of lungs.

Every moment is precious. I watch the clock. Soon I will have to pick up the pieces on the floor. Dress myself. But later, I keep telling myself. Later we'll have all the time in the world.

"Does time slow down in the desert?" I ask him.

"My time away from here went so fast."

"You were just waiting to get back to me."

I feel Jay smiling, the lips pulling up against my forehead.

"When we leave here, time will stand still." I say it even though I don't know what I mean. I've never wanted time to stand still before. It's always been *rush rush rush* toward leaving. I close my eyes and I see Danny, standing alone. It jerks at my soul and so I push it away.

"Are you coming with me? When I leave." Asking the question for real.

Silence and then Jay says, "Yes." A whisper, but it's there. One word. *Yes.*

20

"Girls will wear white. White dress or skirt and blouse, please, and white shoes. And boys will wear black. Dress pants and shoes."

"Jeez, it's like we're getting married. Little brides and grooms."

Ginny laughs at my comment, but I can see that she's not really paying attention. Something is on her mind.

"No sneakers, mind you. No T-shirts. Think of this as a formal affair. Over the next few days, you should all be fitted for your caps and gowns. Times are posted on the wall next to my office."

Old Man Jenkins finishes his announcement and leaves the podium. That means we're free to go. I follow Ginny out to her car. I'm ready to talk, bursting with my news about Jay. But Ginny keeps looking off toward the edge of the parking lot like she's waiting for someone to show up. Taylor, I guess. Maybe she's afraid of running into him. I don't think she's played out the breakup scene yet. He keeps following her around the halls with these big puppy dog eyes. I feel bad for him, but not bad enough to intervene.

"Two weeks to go," I say, instead of jumping in with my future plans. "Can you believe it?"

A half smile flits across Ginny's face.

"Have you made the decision?"

She seems startled for a moment. "What do you mean?"

"About prom? Who's it going to be? Reid or Taylor?"

She shakes her head, looks away. I keep talking.

"Well you've only got a week. You're going to have to make a decision soon."

Ginny looks down and suddenly reaches out for my wrist. She holds it, fingering the beads she gave me. Her face is paper white. She usually has a starter tan going by now, but her skin is pale, the eyes a little red around the edges. If I didn't know better I would think she'd been crying. But I can't imagine what she'd be crying about. Then she tells me.

"Lu." She comes in closer. "Lu, I'm pregnant."

I start to grin because I think she's joking with me, but when her eyes don't meet mine, I know she's telling the truth.

"Gin," I say, because I can't think of anything else. She keeps holding on to my wrist. "Gin, I thought—" I let the words stop because I know it sounds like an accusation.

"You thought I was always real careful, right?" She lets go, shrugs, backs away. "Accidents happen, you know?"

168

"I know, but shit. Gin." I can't seem to find the right things to say. "What are you going to do?"

A blast of music cuts off her words. We both look toward the far end of the parking lot. The marching band is starting practice, playing some rah-rah tune. Ginny watches them for a minute.

"I'm thinking about having it," she says in a quiet voice. At first I don't think I've heard right over the noise. I cock my head to one side and Ginny nods. "I'm thinking about having it, Lu."

I stare at her, speechless, hunting around for some kind of direction. I remember her doctor's wife fantasy, but I can't believe she really wants to make it come true. "But Gin, you know, we're not living in the Dark Ages. There are options."

Ginny nods but I'm not sure she's really listening.

"Have you told Reid?"

Her nod changes direction. "No, but we're real serious."

I keep staring at her. I'm trying to think of ways to reason with her logic.

"You hate the idea, don't you, Lu?" Ginny asks. "I mean, you want to leave here as quick as you can. You hate the idea of anything tying you down."

"We're just getting out of high school, Gin. I would think you'd feel the same way."

"Sometimes I do, but sometimes—" Another loud blast from the brass section cuts off her words. I wait, but her face smooths out and she raises her chin. Presto chango, she's almost the Ginny I know. "I've got to go now. I'll call you later."

She's starting to spin away, but I catch her.

"Promise?"

Ginny laughs—her old laugh. "I'll call you later," she says again.

I stand still, watching the Porsche take off, weaving around the other departing seniors. It gets stopped at the mouth of the parking lot, waiting for the marching band to pass by. Ginny leans out the window to call to some of the band members. I reach for my camera and focus. She seems to feel it and turns back toward me, her blond hair whipping into the air in a sudden breeze. She doesn't smile, just watches me for a few seconds and I click.

The band passes by and Ginny slips back inside. The car disappears around the bend.

21

"Fries or baked potato?"

Sometimes I ask the question in my sleep, I swear, dreaming of giant, bloody steaks that get up and walk around like the live animals they used to be. I could actually do this job in my sleep, but it won't be long now. A finite amount of time I have left to put on my uniform and act all sweet and helpful.

"Would you like butter or sour cream on that, ma'am?"

Wednesday night is church night in this town. Everybody's ready to chow down after a few hours of praying. My section is full and they just keep coming. There aren't a lot of fine dining choices in

Rainey. The Steakhouse is what people around here call quality, which really means a lot of food for your money. If I never see another steak again, it won't kill me. It amazes me what people can cram down their throats and still be able to get up and walk out the door.

I'm serving a big party when I notice Taylor and Wade are my new two-top.

"They tried to seat us somewhere else," Wade explains when I set down their waters. "But I just had to wait for you. I like the idea of you serving me."

"Yeah, well, you better be ready because I don't have time for fun and games."

"You better be good to us, Lu," Wade answers. "Otherwise I won't give you a big fat tip."

I take their order, but I get the busboy to bring them bread and Cokes. Later, after they've eaten and Wade has gotten up to go to the bathroom, Taylor waves me over.

"What's going on with Ginny?" Taylor asks. "She won't talk to me."

I shake my head. "You know I don't get involved."

"There's somebody else, isn't there? That guy she took off with."

I keep clearing the plates, stacking them on my tray.

"I just don't understand why she won't talk to me."

I think about Ginny—laughing after our near collision, dancing until she can hardly stand. I was wrong about her in a way. I didn't think anything could hold her down.

"You know you missed your chance." It's Wade, back in full force, brushing up against me.

"What chance was that?"

"I'm going to the prom with Stacy Lawry."

"I'm very happy for you, Wade."

"Had to ask somebody, this late in the game."

I nod my head, relieved. I'm just about gone, but Wade's words stop me.

"Are you going to get your old man to take you?"

"What are you talking about? You mean my dad?"

Wade grins, happy that I'm taking the bait.

"That old guy you're hanging out with these days. Biker Joe."

This time I'm too surprised to get angry. But I guess it was only a matter of time. More people catching sight of us riding around. Even if we're careful. It's like the town is made of eyes and mouths, just waiting to see something to talk about.

For once I don't have any comeback for Wade. I just stare at him and then I walk away. Wade knows he got to me.

"I figure it's a good thing," he says when I come back around with their check. "You'll get tired of old meat, and come around to see what you've been missing."

I keep quiet. Taylor gives me a pleading look, still trying to get me to give him the lowdown on Ginny.

"There *is* somebody else, Taylor." I say it and I know I'm talking out of spite. "I'd give her up if I were you."

I turn away so I don't have to see his face. I stay

busy with my other tables and when I check, they've already gone, leaving a few wadded-up bills for me.

After the rush everything quiets down. The holy rollers like to eat and hurry home to their TV shows and early bed. I take a break and go out behind the Dumpster to get high with a couple of the cooks. They're always holding some killer stuff, and for the rest of the night, I'm floating along, waiting for punch-out time. I start refilling the salt and pepper shakers and the ketchup bottles. A mindless task, but good for my soul right now.

I keep going in circles around Ginny. I see her turning into her mama, with the perfect house to keep, the kids, the doctor coming home to a couple of martinis or bourbon on the rocks, weekends spent at the club. The whole thing makes me feel alone. Am I the only one who wants to leave this place?

But no, Jay wants to leave too, with me. It doesn't matter if Wade knows about Jay, if the whole town knows. I'm as good as gone. And so is Jay.

Out in the parking lot, after I've punched out,

the air is still warm. I wonder what it's like out west. It must stay hot all year long. On the way home I keep the windows rolled down, the night air rushing in and waking me up. I feel a tingling in my body. A new excitement. Jay is going with me. He said yes. We have plans to make.

When I turn into the drive, my father's spot is empty. I sit for a while in the dark after I've cut the engine. I know he must be with Melanie right now. The injustice of it all hits me. My father is at least ten years older than Melanie, maybe fifteen. But nobody says a word about that.

Inside Jay's cabin I can't get out of my clothes fast enough, the smell of meat and grease falling away from me in a heap.

"You're so small," Jay whispers against my neck. "Sometimes I'm afraid you'll break."

I look down at his hand flat against my stomach and I can't help but think of Ginny. Accidents happen. But not here. Jay and I have been careful.

I would never do anything to hurt you.

176

Jay's words. Words I trust.

"Don't worry," I tell him now. "I'm pretty strong." I flex my muscles as a joke but I do feel strong. Invincible. I feel like a giantess. I have my whole life ahead of me, as Jay said. I pull him into me. Interlocking pieces. A perfect fit.

Afterward, when we can talk again, I want to start making plans. Jay hesitates when I try to pin it down. Liftoff. He says he should finish up the job he's doing with Danny. That will take him through to a couple of weeks after graduation. I feel disappointed. I had visions of taking off the day after walking down the graduation aisle, but I tell myself I can wait. What's a few more weeks? If my father gives me a hard time, I can pay him rent for my room. I could even stay at the Bide-a-Wee if I need to. I think Gran Mac would understand. I could work at the Steakhouse another couple of weeks to save more cash.

"Your dad's not going to be too thrilled."

"It doesn't matter. Nothing matters anymore."

Jay is silent. I know he's thinking about Danny.

"It'll be all right. Danny will come around."

Jay nods his head, but I can tell he's still working through it.

"Danny's going to miss you."

"I know." I keep seeing his face from the other day. I feel sad but I still feel angry too.

"Your dad's going to miss you too."

"Yeah, right. I think he'll be relieved to have me out of his hair. He won't have to worry about me anymore."

"I think he'll still worry."

I turn away from Jay. I don't understand how he can stick up for my father when my father says such terrible things about him, gets Danny to spy on us.

"He has Melanie now. Can you believe it? After all this time he goes after some ditz in his office."

"He's lonely. He needs somebody."

For some reason this sends me up and out of bed. The idea of my father lonely and needing somebody is too much for me to take lying down.

"I don't think he needs anything. He's totally self-sufficient."

I begin to dress and Jay reaches out to catch me.

"You can be really hard on people, Lu. Like I said before, you have to decide if you're going to use your anger or if your anger is going to use you."

"Sounds like you've been reading self-help books in your spare time." The words are out before I can stop them. Jay releases me. He lies back in the sheets. I can feel him watching me.

"I'm sorry," I say, without turning toward him. "It's just that things are getting to me. It's this small town. Everything will be different when we're out of here."

I turn and Jay is looking off, over my head. I want him to agree with me that everything will be different. But he doesn't say a word. I kiss him and leave the cabin, walk back through the shadowy trees. My father's car is still gone.

22

Over the next couple of days I try to find Ginny, but I keep missing her between classes and when I call she's not at home. On Friday night I head over to Lexington to see Orpheus play their biggest gig yet: the Kat Klub. It's a good crowd, but the band isn't grooving. There's no smiling back and forth between Danny and Jay. The music is spotless, but there's no life. The wives are listless, watching the band, sipping at their drinks. Lena leans into me at one point and gives me a sly look.

"I hope you know what you're getting into," she says.

I stare back at her—the killer stare. Her eyes go wide and she pulls away.

Only Teresa makes idle small talk. She smiles at me and asks me questions about school and what Danny was like when he was a little boy. It hits me how similar she and Melanie are. It seems that both my father and brother are into mindless talkers. I

start seeing them as more and more alike.

When there's a break, the band scatters. No sitting at the wives' table. No grouping out in the parking lot passing a joint.

Danny nods in my direction, but that's all. I tell myself it doesn't matter. I ignore this feeling gnawing at my insides. I've never known what it's like to be out of Danny's sunshine ray of love.

Jay positions himself at the far end of the bar and I follow. He has his shades on, and I want to reach out and take them off, but I can tell he doesn't want the contact. Suddenly I feel like he's blaming me, for the band's bad night. I feel like they're all blaming me.

The next set is more jumbled. There are a couple of false starts. The crowd starts to dwindle. At one point I catch Danny glaring at Jay, angry over some missed beat. When Jay steps up to sing his song, Danny doesn't smile. He stares off to one side as he beats out the rhythm.

I stay until the last song, thinking Jay will follow me home. But he tells me that he's going to hang out a little longer with Tom.

"You're okay, right? To drive home?"

"I'm always okay," I answer. I can't help but notice as I'm leaving. Tom is sitting at a table with a couple of blondes.

I take it fast. All the way home. I feel black inside. As black as the moonless night around me. And somehow I'm not surprised to see my father's car in the drive, lights on all over the house. It figures. Everything out of sync tonight. I take a deep breath before I open the front door. I know I'm in for a shit fest. I'm ready for the fight.

Inside the kitchen my father is standing at the counter, a bottle of whiskey and an empty glass in front of him.

"Where have you been?" he asks.

"Danny had a gig," I answer.

"It's two o'clock in the morning!"

"Since when do you care what time I get home? It's not like you've been around much lately."

My father lurches forward, and I realize he's drunk. It's the first time I've ever seen him this way.

He towers over me, his face red, his eyes watery.

"You still live in this house."

"Not for long," I say, and then I see past my father's body to the table. Black-and-white photographs are strewn across the surface. My photos. Of Jay.

I can't say anything. I rush to the table and begin to shuffle the images together, my hands shaking with my anger.

"All this time, I gave that pervert a place to stay. And he had one thing on his mind. Danny said he'd changed. But he hasn't changed. Still chasing everything that moves. All this time, he was talking nice to me, paying me rent, just so he could get into your pants."

I keep my back to him. I feel invaded, dirty. My father delving into my world, looking at the photos, looking at my life. There are no naked photos of me here, but there might as well be.

"I'm going to call the sheriff, have that pervert arrested."

"For what?" I whirl around. "I'm not a minor

anymore. I'm eighteen if you recall. You can't touch me."

"Oh, but that pervert can?"

"He can do whatever he wants."

I feel the slap before I'm even conscious of my father raising his arm. A red-hot stinging. But I don't move away or cry. I stand staring at him, my eyes cold as steel. He slaps me once, twice, I begin to lose count. Each time I raise my chin and face him again, which seems to make him more angry. He keeps going. My cheek is beginning to throb, but I won't cry. Finally I catch his arm.

"Hit me again, and I'm the one who's going to call the cops."

My father blinks a few times and then staggers backward. He looks down at his hands and back at me, flushed and in shock. I wonder if he even knew he was hitting me.

I gather the photos together and head for the basement, locking the door behind me. Some photos have been ripped from the walls and scattered on the floor. Not just Jay, but photos of Ginny and hangout scenes. Only my self-portrait wall is still intact. I run my hands over my paper face. And this is where I start to cry. Great sobs that rack my whole body. I finish the job my father started. Ripping at the photos of myself. I bring them to my face. Salt water rinsing over the paper.

23

I wake up and at first I don't know where I am. Heavy dark even though I know it's morning. Cold floor against skin. I look around and the photos are scattered everywhere, some of them covering me like a blanket. I know I need to get up and warn Jay against my father's wrath, but I can't move yet. My cheek feels swollen from where my father hit me. I stand up and go to the mirror. There's no bruise or mark, but the skin is tender.

Upstairs the house is quiet. I rush outside and down the road. Jay's bike is there. The door is open. Jay is already putting things in boxes. I stand in the doorway and watch him. Finally he looks up.

"Are you okay?" he asks.

I can't answer right away. I don't know if I'm okay.

"We knew this might happen, Lu. I'm not surprised your dad flipped."

I walk farther into the room. The guitar is propped up against the couch. I run my hand over the strings.

"It doesn't matter. It doesn't change anything," I say.

Jay lets out a long breath and looks down at his hands.

"It doesn't change anything. My dad flipping out." I move closer until he can't help but look at me. The gray eyes looking deep into me like they did that first night when I recognized him after so many years.

"We need to let things settle down."

I shake my head. "We could take off now. Today."

"You've got graduation."

"It doesn't matter."

Jay runs a finger gently down my cheek and I flinch a little.

"It *does* matter. This is your life, Lu. It's not a game."

It's the first time since we started this that I feel the distance, the years between us. An old man giving a lecture.

"Maybe you're the one who's been playing games." I can't look at him as I say it.

His arms drop to his sides. "Like I said, we should let things settle, let your dad cool down."

I watch him go back to packing up. "Where are you going to be?"

"Tom said I could crash with him for a while."

I look around the room. Not much more to go. It's not like he brought a lot with him when he moved in.

Outside the door I start to run. It's like my lungs have stopped functioning and I need to jump-start them. My father is still absent, vacating the premises after causing the explosion. My first impulse is to call Danny, but then I remember. They're on the same side. I try Ginny, but she doesn't have time to talk.

"I'm telling Reid today. Wish me luck."

"Luck," I say, but the line is already dead.

Inside my room I start packing a bag. Just the basics. Something stops me from going into the darkroom. I don't think I can take all the photos lying in piles across the floor. I throw everything into the Nova and head toward Bide-a-Wee. My father must have told Gran Mac something because she doesn't ask me any questions. She shows me to the guest room in her apartment.

"It will be nice having company," she says, and I try to smile. She goes back to sit behind the counter and I fall on the oversoft twin bed. Instantly I'm asleep.

When I wake again, I hear voices. I go to the window and move the shade an inch. My father's car is in the lot. I can hear his voice, but I can't make out the words. Then Gran says, "She can stay here as long as she likes." My father says something else and then he walks to the car and opens the door. He turns and glances up at the window, but I know he can't see me.

24

A whole day passes without Jay. And then another and another. I go through the motions. Get fitted for my cap and gown. I look through Gran's closet and find one of her old cream-colored dresses. The shoes I find at the Goodwill. Somebody's old wedding shoes, discarded.

At night I run my hands over my body. Withdrawal. That's what it is. From Jay. I can't believe he's not feeling it too. This need to have our bodies together.

Gran loves cooking me breakfast in the morning. She tries to wait up for me after my shift at the Steakhouse. I work at being a good little girl for her sake, but I spend most of my days high. Lighting up inside the car, airing out before I come home to Gran.

Ginny is like a ghost. I keep following her traces. She's ditching school and all the regular places. I wait for her to call, tell me how it went with Reid. I wait for Jay to call. But the only people calling Bide-a-Wee are the occasional tourists asking for directions.

When my stash gets low, I head toward Rounders. Bunny is happy to see me.

"Thought you'd forgotten about your old friend," he says when he has me in his grasp. He sells me a dime bag and then something makes me ask him about the stuff I tried before.

"So you liked that little taste," he says, smiling his slithery smile, the forked tongue darting in and out.

I know I'm like a fish on the line, but I want something more than grass. This time without Jay. I need something to totally numb the senses.

Bunny takes my money and gives me a small bottle of pills.

"Hey, I thought you were hanging out with Shepard," he says as I'm about to leave.

I stop and wait for the news. I feel like there must be a billboard announcing my life to the whole town. "The thing is, I saw him last night. Over at Calhoun's. He was with another chick."

A punch in the stomach. All the wind knocked out of me. That's the way it feels. But I try not to give Bunny the satisfaction of knowing he has dealt some kind of mortal blow. Payback for not joining his illustrious blow-job club. I turn and head for the car.

One little white pill makes my shift all muddy. I keep forgetting orders and Lottie, one of the old-time waitresses, has to keep covering

"You're lucky Ron isn't here tonight," she tells me at the coffee station.

"It doesn't matter." I shrug. "I'm out of here. Coupla weeks, I'm history."

"Honey, that's what I was always saying when I was your age."

"What happened?" Suddenly I want to know Lottie's life story. What kept her here in Rainey.

"Life happened. Isn't that a T-shirt or something?

Shit happens? I got pregnant, I got married, I got stuck."

I watch Lottie's face—the lines that make her look fifty when she's probably not much over thirty—and I'm seeing Ginny. As soon as I punch out, I drive to her house. Her window is dark. I sit watching it, wondering how things change so fast. Ginny, me and Jay—we were all cruising in high gear and then suddenly—click down—and we've slammed into neutral.

25

When Gran Mac asks what I'm doing Friday night, I tell her I'm hanging out with Ginny. I watch the worry pass over her face. I promise myself I'll be home early for her sake.

In the Kat Klub parking lot, I pop another pill, wait behind the wheel for it to take effect. Through the doors the club is heavy with smoke. The stage is empty. The band must be taking their first break.

The wives nod, but they don't smile or pull me into their conversation. Teresa isn't there. Danny must be out back. I stick to the corners, watching for Jay. When I find him, I want to cry out. He is sitting at a table and he is not alone. A woman is with him, her body pressed against his arm.

How long did that take?

I must ask the question out loud because the couple next to me glances in my direction.

Crazy. I want to tell them. Crazy Lu.

I stay hidden until the break is over. The guys take their places and the music begins. I feel this hunger when I look at Jay. I can't help it. Like I'm starving, haven't eaten in days. I know every inch of his body now, but he seems so far away, up on stage, untouchable, the lights holding him sacred and godlike.

The drug in my veins makes me want to move and so I start to dance at the edge of the crowd. I close my eyes and think of Ginny. I want her here with me, dancing like we always do. When I open my eyes, there's a guy closing in. It feels like Ginny

193

is taking me over. I imagine myself a magnet and the guy sticks. We move deeper into the crowd, my body writhing close. Every song. I keep dancing. I don't want to stop. This motion. The music turns slow and I let strange arms wrap around me. When I glance up, I know Jay is watching me. I want him to watch, see what he's missing.

I lose track of time. The world starts to become clearer, more defined. The colors inside the dark room become bolder and leap out, envelop me. In a rush it feels like I can't breathe. I leave my stranger hanging and stumble my way through the crowd.

Outside the night air shoots into my lungs. Every breath is painful. I get behind the wheel and wait, concentrate on taking in air. I don't know how long I sit, but when I look up, Jay's face is there in the open window.

"What's going on, Lu?" he asks. His gray eyes are like pools of dead-still water. I want to dive in and swim around inside his brain, touch what he's thinking.

"I could ask you the same thing."

He cocks his head. No familiar smile to soften his confusion. "What are you talking about?"

"It's a small town, Jay." I feel like I'm the one who needs to enlighten him. I am telling him a great truth. "Things get around. No matter how you try to hide them."

"I don't have anything to hide."

He holds his hands out, palms up, and I want to take those hands and put them on my body, stop the trembling that's started to roll through me.

"Wait for me," Jay says. "You can leave your car here. I'll drive you home."

I shake my head and rev the engine. "I'm tired of waiting."

Jay takes a step back and I shoot out of the parking lot. It seems like I'm driving through water. I know the car is moving because I can check the speedometer, but I swear it's like I'm floating. The car lights coming at me are like bright flowers in a dark pool. I'm moving in between the flowers, trying to stay on the right path. I know the next curve will bring me to the halfway mark, but then I'm slamming on the brakes, jolting to a stop behind a long line of red dots.

I lean out the window and squint down the road of stopped cars. There's a police car up ahead. I can see the red and blue lights zinging off the trees. I think it must be a roadblock, cops checking for boozers and stoners, so I shove my pills and my pot into this hollowed-out place inside the door. I rummage through my bag for gum, something to mask my breath. But then someone is talking close by and I catch the word "accident." I look up again and people are outside their cars, trying to get a better view. I open the door and step onto blacktop. The air is tinged with smoke.

"It's that bad stretch," the man in front of me is saying.

"The kids call it 'Dead Man,'" the woman next to him adds.

The man turns to look at me, shading his eyes against the glare from my headlights.

"You better switch your blinkers on, hon," he calls, and I nod and obey just in time. A car comes around the curve and catches us all. Deer in the headlights. The man ahead of me takes control, walking down to give the new arrivals the scoop.

"Probably some kids," the man is saying. "Going to Huntsville." There's a murmur of agreement.

"They oughta straighten out this road," a woman's voice says.

"They've been talking about that for years," the man answers.

Up ahead there's a small white light moving in the dark. Every so often the light disappears and a red flare ignites on the ground. Everyone is quiet, waiting. It's a trooper placing emergency lights to guide the way.

"What's going on, officer?" somebody asks.

The cop shakes his head and keeps lighting his flares. "We need you folks to be patient just a little while longer" is all he says.

But everybody knows now it's a car, spinning off the turn. The word comes down from the front of the line. And then there's a sound in the distance. Thin and long, piercing the dark.

It's not like I haven't heard ambulances over the years, but this one—the way it comes out of nowhere, winding through the trees, rushing faster and faster straight for us—takes me into the past. I put my hands over my ears, close my eyes, but I can't drown out the sound. The ambulance roars by and stops. A moment of silence. And then it's flashing past again, even louder this time. A terrible wailing. Something that can't be stopped, can't be shut out.

"Hey, sugar, you okay?"

I know the man is talking to me, so I open my eyes, let my hands fall to my sides. I nod my head even though I don't feel okay. I feel like something has come undone, unraveled with the sound of the ambulance. My hands are shaking again and I want to be home now, even though I don't know where home is. Images pop into my head. Photographs I've taken. Bide-a-Wee. Jay's bedroom. My father's house. My mother's garden.

Back inside the car I wait for the line to creep

forward. Everybody's going slow, trying to get a good glimpse of the crime scene. Dead Man itself is lit up like Christmas. Huge cop lights making everything clear. The car is still there, lying flipped on one side, half of it sticking out from the ditch that runs alongside the road. A fire truck is nearby, firefighters rolling up their hoses. The smell of smoke is strong. Burned-out metal. The car is blackened, charred beyond recognition, except that I think I recognize something. The shape, the bits of cherry red still visible through the black.

I feel sick, dizzy, but I grip the wheel and hold on tight until I'm in the dark again. I know the pills I've been taking make me hallucinate. I know I must be hallucinating now. I tailgate the car ahead until the WELCOME TO RAINEY sign and then I speed past, blast through the lights.

At Ginny's house I see the cop car in the driveway. Ginny's father is standing on the porch, talking with an officer. It seems to take years for me to walk across the lawn. My legs are moving, but it feels like

I'm standing still. When I get to the steps, the men stop talking and turn to look at me.

"Lulu," Mr. Cavanaugh says. He looks around as if he's confused about something. "Ginny isn't here."

I take a step forward and the officer reaches out and takes hold of my shoulder. A strong grip as if he knows I'm going to try to run away.

"Are you Lulu McClellan?" he asks.

"I was on the road—" I try to explain. "I saw—"

"Your father is looking for you," the officer continues. "He thought you were with Miss Cavanaugh."

"Where is she? Where's Ginny?" I know. I know already. But I have to ask.

"Ginny isn't here," Mr. Cavanaugh says again, his eyes watching me from miles away. "She's gone."

26

Photographs. They're still scattered across the floor when I make it home. Some of them are crumpled or creased. I kneel down and try to flatten them out with the palms of my hands.

ginny: catching a breeze

ginny: getting crazy

ginny: hitting the hard stuff

When I have a neat pile, I begin to tape them to the wall, the way they used to be. My gallery. My shrine.

My father stands at the top of the stairs and watches me. Melanie is with him. She peeks over his shoulder, and I know she wants to speak. But neither of them says a word. I guess the cop called to warn them I was on my way. My father was waiting for me at the door. He reached out his hands to me, but I kept walking, down the stairs, into what was once my private world.

It takes hours to sort through them all, tape them back into their places. At first I try to stay chronological. The passing of time. But then I just go to the random. Ginny at sixteen to Ginny just a few months ago.

When I'm finished, I slide down against the wall opposite and stay there, watching the light change. The sun comes in through the small window above the sink. My eyelids are heavy but I don't want to sleep. I don't want to dream of colors and wailing sounds and burned-out hunks of metal. I don't want to dream at all.

At some point there are footsteps on the stairs. Somebody coming down into the depths to try to retrieve me. It's Danny, kneeling down, taking my hand, calling my name.

"You're not supposed to look at me," I whisper, and my voice is strange in my ears. "Don't you know? If you want to bring me back, you're not supposed to look at me."

"What are you talking about, Lu?" Danny asks in a gentle voice.

But I just shake my head. Danny notices the wall. He gets up and stands in front of it, examining the facts of Ginny's life.

Then he comes back to me. "I'm sorry, Lu. Not just

about this." His hand gestures toward the photographs. "I'm sorry about stepping in where I don't belong, misjudging things."

I shrug. "Maybe you didn't. Misjudge. Anyway, it doesn't matter." I stare up at the photographs. How can anything matter when there's always death around some turn, waiting, waiting for just the right moment?

27

Days pass. I know this because the sun goes up and down. People come and go. Danny, Gran Mac, my father. I leave the basement, but it still feels like I'm down below, moving through shadows. Melanie cooks me things and puts them in front of me, but I can't eat. I start popping the pills like candy. They keep everything at a distance. Nothing is real. At school there's a candlelight vigil and a pilgrimage out to Dead Man to leave flowers and cards. I hear about these things, but I don't participate.

At the funeral I sit behind the Cavanaughs and think about luck and fate. Tragic. That's what people will see when they look at this family. Two children lost so young. Fast living. Speedboats and sports cars. A tragic end.

Mr. Cavanaugh stares straight ahead at the closed casket, but Mrs. Cavanaugh watches her hands. I can't say a word to her when it's time to give the condolences. I watch her blank, perfectly madeup face and know she's just as high as I am. Bunny's little white pills for me. For her, probably Valium or something stronger that her doctor prescribed. Something to get her through this day. As I'm about to move past, she suddenly grabs my arm the way Ginny used to do. She's staring at the beads around my wrist.

"Ginny gave them to me," I tell her.

She fingers the beads, her face wrinkling up. For a minute I think she's going to break down. But it passes and her face goes blank again.

"Good," she says, patting my hand. "I'm glad."

I pass by the coffin like you're supposed to do,

but I can't touch it. I can't wrap my mind around what's inside. I keep seeing her, on that Sunday night ride we took together. I keep hearing the gasp and seeing the headlights flashing. The moment of fear before Ginny got control again. I keep wondering if that's what it was like. The last few seconds. If Ginny knew. If she saw it all before her.

Outside I am blind in the sun. Another hand shoots out and grabs me. Taylor's face comes close. His eyes are bloodshot, his breath smells like whiskey.

"What they're saying, is it true?" he asks me.

I stare at him, not understanding. He pulls me away from the crowd of mourners.

"They're saying she was pregnant." Taylor leans in closer. "It wasn't me, so it had to be that guy. That guy she was seeing." He looks around. "Where is he? Where is he now?"

I follow Taylor's gaze and it's true. Gin's college boy is nowhere to be seen. I feel a shot of anger and I push away from Taylor, turn my back on him and keep walking toward my father's car. The anger just keeps building. Anger at this town for spreading gossip so fast; anger at Reid for getting Ginny into trouble. And then I'm angry at Ginny herself. Blindfolded. That's what she said. She said she could take that road blindfolded. She said she was invincible. And I believed her.

My father drives me home, but I can't stay inside. The anger keeps me walking, down to the lake, through the woods, into Jay's cabin. The rooms are empty and I can't feel it anymore. The aching, the heat. It seems like years ago. I follow the road back home, back to my mother's garden. The first spring flowers are gone and now there are hydrangeas and fuchsias and cosmos. The roses are still in bloom. Bloodred and prickly.

I sit down among the colors. Red and purple, yellow and green. And blue—high above—the sky is an endless blue. I stare into the colors and I begin to see her there. Her long dark hair piled up on top of her head against the heat, her body crouched down so that she is the same size as me. She is weeding her garden, pulling at the unwanted roots.

She hums while she works, a tune I like, one that rocks me to sleep at night. And then the humming stops. She begins to turn and I think she is turning toward me, but it's like some invisible string yanks at her and she is falling, falling into the flowers, crumpling them beneath her weight.

At first I think she is playing a game, and so I wait. I wait a long time. Yellow butterflies come and land on her shoulders, in her hair. Finally I move toward her, slowly and quietly, sneaking up on her so as to startle her back into motion. I crouch and put my whole body around hers and now, even now, in the heat, in the passing of years, I can feel the cold. Her body so cold. So quiet and so still. And that's when I start to scream. A cry loud enough to bring Danny.

But it's not Danny this time. It's my father. Kneeling down beside me, holding me, wrapping me up. The way I remember it from long ago, snug inside his arms.

I don't know how long we sit there, rocking together. In the quiet I hear his voice. It sounds far away even though his mouth is pressed against my ear.

"I thought it was you. On the news. The car crash. I thought it was you. You told Gran you were with her that night. And I thought you were in the car with her."

"I should have been," I say, and I feel his head shaking.

"You're just like your mother. So tiny. I always wanted to protect her. But I couldn't. I knew I couldn't protect you either."

I let him hold me tighter. I do not pull away. But I know what he's saying is true. There is no protection in this world. No guarantee. I don't feel safe in his arms. I don't feel safe here in my mother's garden. I wonder why I ever wanted to go into the wider world where there are even more dangers. I wonder why I ever wanted to leave at all.

28

"We will now have a moment of silence for Virginia Emily Cavanaugh, who is no longer with us."

That's what it comes down to. At graduation. A few seconds of silence. And when time is up, a word about the future and a great yell. Caps thrown into the air. Nobody wants to think about death too long. Everybody here wants to believe they will live forever.

At home Gran Mac and Melanie and Teresa bustle around the kitchen, preparing a celebration dinner. I watch them from the deck through the sliding glass door. Gran keeps saying how happy she is to have two women in her two men's lives.

It's awkward with my father after the garden scene. It's not like everything has gone back to being the way it was before I started being his problem child. It's just that he's more careful now. He speaks very slowly to me, as if I am from another country. And maybe I am. I haven't picked up the camera in weeks, but I still can't help being the one on the outside, watching.

"What are your plans now, Lulu?"

It's Melanie who asks the question at the table. The question I'm sure they've all been dying to ask.

Everyone stops their eating to look at me.

"The manager said I could keep my shift at the Steakhouse," I hear myself say. "Maybe I'll take some classes at UK."

"Photography classes?" Teresa asks. "Danny tells me you're really good at it."

I shrug and watch my fork move food around my plate.

"Maybe your father could teach you the business," Melanie says, and her voice is so bright I have to squint when I answer the question.

"Maybe so."

When the meal is over, I leave the women cleaning up in the kitchen. I go to the garden and sit. This is what I do most of the time now. I want to put my hands in the dirt, but the gardener keeps everything so perfect, I'd be afraid of messing something up.

Danny comes to find me. He doesn't say anything right away. We sit listening to the cicadas and the beginning of the nightingale's song.

"Jay has been asking about you," Danny says.

I feel a tiny burst of something, but it's gone

right away. I like to keep everything on one level these days. No ups for sure. But no downs either.

"I thought about asking him to come by tonight for dinner, but I didn't know how you'd feel."

I pull at some dead leaves on the rosebush and watch them crumble in my hand.

"The band—we're grooving again. You should come check us out. We're playing at the Kat Klub again in a couple of weeks."

I nod my head, but I doubt I'll go. It's too painful. When I think of Orpheus playing, I think of Ginny. That first night Jay took over the stage. If I had held on to Ginny then, if I hadn't let go to rush into Jay's world, she might still be here, in this one. Crazy maybe. Crazy Lu. But I keep going back to that moment when I let her slip away. Now it seems pointless to hold on to anything.

Danny keeps trying to have a conversation, but I keep concentrating on the flowers around me. After a while he runs a hand down my back and leaves.

Everything is quiet by the time I come back to the house. I can hear the muffled sound of Melanie and my father watching TV upstairs. I head to my own room and night merges into day. I keep a steady high going between the pills and the pot. I do my job, sometimes working a double shift so that I don't have to think about anything except whether somebody wants baked or fried and how rare they want their meat.

During the day when I'm not at Bide-a-Wee, I sit out on the deck in the sun. I'm getting darker and darker. A brown bean, Melanie calls me. Slowly Melanie is taking over the house, making it feel inhabited. Furniture gets rearranged and the kitchen is full of cooking smells. Her presence grows larger and mine grows smaller, until one afternoon I pack some things and take them down to the cabin. When my father gets home, he comes to inspect the transfer of goods. He nods his head without saying anything. I wonder if he's thinking it's the natural flow of events. The McClellans leaving home but not venturing too far.

The first night alone in the cabin I lie on the bed in the dark and think of Jay. His hands on my body.

His gray eyes watching my reaction as he touched me. I can look at it all as if from a great distance. As if it's something that happened long ago.

When I'm low on my stash I head to Rounders. Bunny is ultrapolite. He doesn't try any funny stuff. I seem to be immune from any real one-on-one. I hang around and get high with Alix and Darrell sometimes, but that's my only outside contact. Otherwise it's just Melanie and my father, Danny and Teresa, Gran Mac, and of course the other servers on my Steakhouse shift.

Danny comes by every few days to make sure I'm still around. He drops information about Jay. How he got a place over on East Main, how he and Danny are working a tough job, a new strip mall on the bypass. But they're still rocking at night. Orpheus is booked up for the summer.

"You should hear us," Danny says. "We got some new songs. I could pick you up next Saturday."

I tell him maybe but when the time comes, I give some excuse. Deep down I know it has to do with staying inside the town limits, staying away from the twists and turns. I'm not sure I could take the road to Hunstville, and beyond to Lexington. I don't want to see the shrine I know is there. The white cross and the faded flowers and the ribbons blowing in the wind.

You're becoming way too solitary.

I hear Ginny talking to me sometimes, telling me things I already know. In my dreams she dances her way through a crowd. I try to reach for her, but she's always one step ahead of me, laughing, turning, waving me closer, only to slip away. Or else she's holding on to me so tight and I'm the one trying to break the grip.

What holds us together? What do you think?

Nothing. Nothing holding us together now. Some-one's always left behind. Someone's always left behind with nothing to hold on to.

29

The summer is a record breaker this year. The heat doesn't let up. It feels like I am sweating down to nothing. In the early mornings and in the evenings I work in my mother's garden. Slowly my father—or more likely Melanie—starts to notice and the gardener stops making his rounds. I pull at the weeds and pinch back the fuchsias and geraniums. I go to the library and pick up books on fertilizing and pest removal and replanting.

After working in the heat I usually jump into the lake and let the dirt wash off my hands and knees and feet. I am becoming a powerful swimmer. I test myself by swimming all the way to the dock in the middle of the lake and back. One evening when the sky is just turning a perfect pink, I come out of the water and I hear a familiar sound. The whine of a bike slowing down, the hum of the motor.

I watch the rippling water, think about hiding, losing myself in the waves. I stand for a long time. Then I wrap the towel around my body, make myself walk back toward the cabin. Jay's bike is parked out front. The door is open and I can hear music coming from inside. It feels like I have shot back through time. The first few weeks, sneaking up on Jay, aching for some kind of sign. I have to remind myself that it's my cabin now. Jay is the intruder.

Silently I walk to the door. He is sitting on the couch, the guitar cradled in the curve of his body. He is concentrating on the song, hasn't seen me yet. The melody is all there. I close my eyes and listen. His voice is soft and tender around the words. Words about love. Something so simple. Love blowing everything else away.

When I open my eyes again, the song is over and Jay is watching me. Everything about him is the same. His face, his eyes, his lips. I drink it in and wonder how everyone else can still be the same when I am so different. Outside and in. I know Jay is noting the differences, just like he did that first night. I know I am even smaller than before, thinner. I am darker and my hair is nearly to my shoulders now. Time flies, Jay told me weeks ago. Time flies when you don't keep track of the days.

"Lu," Jay says. He puts the guitar aside and stands up. "The door was open. I wanted to make sure you're okay. I wanted to—" He reaches out and

I step back, wrap the towel tighter around me. His hands fall to his sides.

"You finished the song," I say.

"I finished it for you," he answers.

I look down at my hands. There is still dirt under the nails. The dirt makes me feel connected to the earth, even when I'm floating, high on my pills. I stand without moving, listening to the sounds outside the cabin. The crickets clicking and the birds getting ready for night.

Jay brushes the strings with one hand then puts the guitar back into its case.

"You know, you were right," I say. "About hiding things."

He cocks his head and waits.

"It's been there all along. My mother. The way it happened. Sometimes I can forget for hours, for days. But it never goes away. It's always there."

Jay comes toward me and I want to hold back, but I can't. Automatic reflex. The body's need to be touched, held. I close my eyes. He wraps me tight in his arms and I can feel a heart beating. It takes me a moment to realize it's my own, beating fast inside my chest. A little bird fluttering, caught in a cage.

The last time. I feel it in my bones. It's like I am watching it all from far away. The end of a love affair. I feel old to know so much. Older than the motion that carries us away. Back onto familiar ground, into the bed where I first felt what it was like to have skin pressed against skin. His hands touching me like I am something precious that will break. And when I feel like I will break, he goes soft and quiet, whispering my name inside the roar.

I close my eyes and let it take me. A tide strong enough to wash away all pain and fear and hesitation.

"I'm sorry," Jay says in the stillness.

"You said you'd never do anything to hurt me. You said that a long time ago. When I was just a little girl."

"I think I loved you. Even back then."

The word love. There between us. The bass line that holds it all together.

"You said you would go with me. To the desert."

"I tried. I tried to tell myself I could. But I can't, Lu. It's not what I can do right now. I started to see that I had to let you go."

You have your whole life ahead of you.

"I don't know if I want to go anymore."

"You have to go."

"But you came back."

Silence. Jay thinking it through.

"Sometimes you have to go away to know what you want. I want to be here for now."

"With me?"

"Yes. If that's what you want. But I don't think it is."

Jay sits up and turns his back to me. I know he's getting ready to leave. I start to reach for the stash of pills I keep beside the bed. I want to make everything unreal.

"What are you doing, Lu?"

He reaches out and grabs my wrist.

"I mean, you're doing what you always said you wouldn't. You're sticking around in a dead-end job, getting high every day, I bet. Living at home. This

219

isn't the desert. This isn't the city. This isn't where you're supposed to be."

His face is turned slightly so I can see the curve of his jaw, the fullness of his lips.

"This isn't what your friend would have wanted. You hanging around, holding on to some ghost."

What holds us together? What do you think?

I look down at Jay's hand wrapped around my flesh and I remember. The way things can be boxed in, separated out, contained. Tiny moments caught on film, on paper. Facts. The facts of my life. The first photograph I took of Jay was of his hands. Large inside the frame. Strong and full of music.

Now I feel the flesh and blood slide away. The skin beneath, my skin, is free of any kind of mark. First time, first love. Cliché, but I feel Jay inside, not outside like some terrible scar. No muffler burns. The kind Jay warned me about. The mangled kind that mark you forever.

I listen to the sounds of his leaving, the bike purring off into the night. I lie back and sleep a dreamless sleep, black as the black inside my dark-room.

In the morning I dress slowly. My head is totally clear for the first time in weeks. I walk down the driveway to the house. At the top of the basement stairs I pause. Someone is down below. I hear the rustle of paper.

My father is sorting through the photographs I left on the floor. There are neat piles on the work table. When he hears me, he turns, and it's not his usual irritated look. It's just that he's caught off guard. His eyes look relieved to see me here. I stand beside him and watch as he keeps flipping through the images.

kentucky roads: highway 27
the singing bridge: graffiti love
alix and darrell: fire it up
huntsville: saturday night
taylor boyd: lost in the brew
rounders: stoner freaks

"These are really good," my father says. He clears his throat. "I can't say I'm always crazy about the subject matter." Pausing at the ones of kids drinking and getting high. I notice there is a pile facedown on the far corner of the table. That must be the photos of Jay. "But you have an eye."

"Camerahead," I whisper. His old nickname for me, not said in niceness.

He seems to wince a little. "I didn't realize." He stops and tries again. "I didn't know how serious you were." He holds up one that took me a lot of time. "I can see how you've worked with this one. Dodging, trying to get the contrast just right."

"How do you know?" I ask.

My father's arm gestures out. "Where do you think all this stuff came from?"

I look around. I found the equipment inside the closet. I found the camera inside a drawer. I never stopped to think about it. I thought it must have been a Danny phase.

"Why did you stop?" I ask.

"Not much money to be made in taking pictures. I had a family to support."

We're silent for a while. Then my father clears his throat and says in a quiet voice, "I was never serious enough about it. And I wasn't as good. As good as you."

I feel something warm inside, spreading through me. I go to the drawer and pull out the photographs of my mother.

"Did you take all these?" I ask.

"Who else?" My father shrugs.

"They're really good."

My father's lips curve up. Something like a smile.

Side by side we go through the pages. Something we have never done together. There are the photos of my mother on her wedding day. Short white dress and long dark hair. There are the photos in Mexico looking like she could stay there forever, blend into the scenery. In all the photos my mother smiles at us from her great distance, and we are forced to smile back. We are the ones left behind, but we are here together. Holding on to memories, holding on to life. I feel my father reaching out to me and I don't turn away. I look from my father's photos to mine. Everything in black and white, but I start to think that maybe I will begin to experiment in color. Reds and purples, yellows and greens. And blue—an endless array of blues to explore.

30

"Dead Man. We're coming up to Dead Man."

I make the announcement to no one but myself. I ease on the brakes and take it slow, pull off the road long before the curve, flip on the blinkers. I sit for a while, breathing in the smell of fresh-cut hay. The summer is almost over and all the farmers are cutting their fields, the hay raked into round bundles like giant jelly rolls. The heat is still in the air. Across the fence a farmer chugs by on his tractor and waves a hand in the air, but he doesn't stop to ask what I'm doing. He's used to it by now, I'm sure. So many people over the years stopping to pay their respects. Not much longer, though. The county has finally decided to straighten out the road. In the *Rainey News* Ginny's name was kept alive all summer.

Let this be the last time we see a young life lost.

I get out of the car and make my way along the edge of the blacktop. There are already little red flags, marking the route the new road will take. In the belly of the curve the white cross is still there. Faded ribbons waving in the breeze. A few dried flower bouquets. There have been so many shrines year to year. I wonder who removes the crosses. I wonder how long they decide is long enough to grieve.

I kneel in the dirt beside the cross and pull out the offering I have brought. Something I'd forgotten about until I found the camera again, saw that there was still half a roll inside. After the negatives had cooked, the frame jumped out at me.

The seniors' lot. Ginny, leaning out her car window. Her face turned back toward me, hair flying free.

ginny: last glance

I take out the tape and attach the photo to the cross. That's all. I don't stay to feel the loss take hold of me again. I know I will always have it in my heart. The way I will always remember what it was like to see my mother die. The way I will always remember what it was like to be touched for the first time. Jay looking at me with desire, with love. I have a long way to go before darkness falls. I have a lot of miles to cover. In the car I have maps and brochures for art schools in New York City. I have the name and address of an old friend of my father's— a place to stay until I'm on my feet. Maybe someday I'll photograph the desert. Maybe someday Jay will meet me there and show me the things he loves— the emptiness, the way the light falls at certain times. But now, I'm on my own, leaving Rainey with nothing but my camera and my photographs and a couple of bags.

After Dead Man the road goes straight and I bring the car back up to speed. The wind coming through the window wipes it all away. Any kind of worry. Without a second thought I slip my hand into my bag. The light coming through the windshield is bright and full of morning. I take my eyes off the road for a split second and snap my own face inside the rearview.

lucinda larrimore mcclellan: making the run